PRAISE FOR WHEN LIFE GIVES YOU MANGOS

AN *OPRAH DAILY* BEST CARIBBEAN BOOK OF THE YEAR

"A heartfelt and accessible debut about friendship, memory, and forgiveness." —Tae Keller, author of Newbery Medal winner *When You Trap a Tiger*

"*When Life Gives You Mangos* is a wonderful story with great heart, mystery, and insight. Kereen Getten is a bright new voice." —Clare Vanderpool, author of Newbery Medal winner *Moon Over Manifest* and Printz Honor book *Navigating Early*

"A heartwarming yet suspenseful debut about the strength of family, the turmoil of friendships lost and found, and most importantly, remembering who you are." —Lynne Kelly, author of Schneider Family Book Award winner *Song for a Whale*

★ "Getten's handling of potentially tough topics like family, disability, and religion is spot-on, weaving important discussions into an adventurous, summery plot that just keeps going." —*School Library Journal*, starred review

★ "Getten lures readers in. . . . Readers occupy pretty much the same position as the island kids, puzzling over clues and gossip but unable to pry out the truth." —*The Bulletin*, starred review

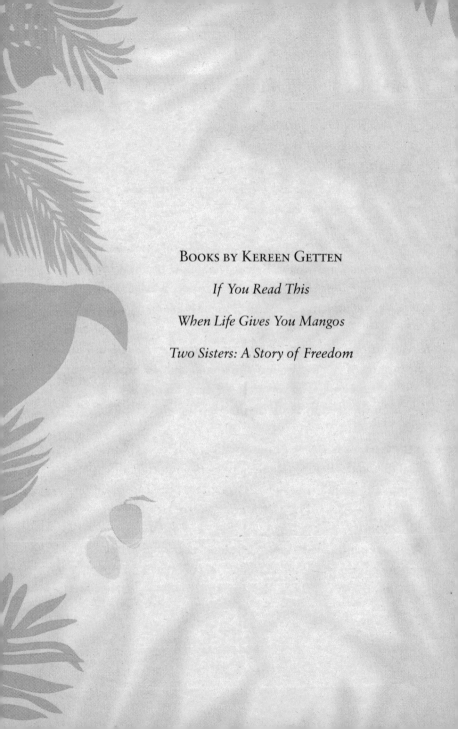

WHEN LIFE GIVES YOU MANGOS

KEREEN GETTEN

A YEARLING BOOK

FOR TRISTAN,
AND THE KIDS WHO DREAM, FOLLOW YOUR HEART.

Text copyright © 2020 by Kereen Getten
Cover art copyright © 2020 by Bex Glendening

All rights reserved. Published in the United States by Yearling, an imprint of Random House Children's Books, a division of Penguin Random House LLC, New York. Originally published in hardcover in the United States by Delacorte Press, an imprint of Random House Children's Books, a division of Penguin Random House LLC, New York, in 2020.

Yearling and the jumping horse design are registered trademarks of Penguin Random House LLC.

Visit us on the Web! rhcbooks.com

Educators and librarians, for a variety of teaching tools, visit us at RHTeachersLibrarians.com

Library of Congress Cataloging-in-Publication Data is available upon request.
ISBN 978-0-593-17397-8 (hc) — ISBN 978-0-593-31021-2 (glb) —
ISBN 978-0-593-17398-5 (ebook) — ISBN 978-0-593-17399-2 (pbk.)

Printed in the United States of America
10 9 8 7 6 5 4 3 2 1
First Yearling Edition 2022

CHAPTER
ONE

THERE IS A NEW GIRL ARRIVING in Sycamore. Her hair is in two Afro buns with big white bows, and she is wearing cat's-eye sunglasses, like a celebrity. That's according to Gaynah. I haven't seen her yet, but Gaynah says she saw her get off the city bus by the traffic circle with a woman that looked like her mother, and they are heading up the hill.

The entire village is buzzing. This is the most excitement we have ever had, and no one wants to miss seeing it for themselves. Within minutes all the kids are gathered at the edge of the road, waiting for the new girl. Everyone is speculating on why she is here and what might be wrong with her.

New people don't come to Sycamore. Not since the witch-doctor episode. The last time someone new came here, it was two tourists with video cameras. They were driving to the Bob Marley museum and got lost. But we suspect they were some of the die-hard fans who were desperate to meet Eldorath, my uncle, the man who saw ghosts.

It's the story that brought shame and fear on the community. Pastor Brown was the most vocal. He said any man who claims to see ghosts is not a godly man, that my uncle was inviting evil to our community. So Eldorath was given a new name: the witch doctor.

Tourists thought differently. My uncle was a tourist attraction. They wanted to see him, ask him if he could see their mother, their father, their best friend who had passed. Uncle Eldorath wasn't easy to find, though; his house was way up on the hill, and he rarely left it. Pastor Brown told us to never give anyone directions.

When they couldn't find him, they gave us candy as a thank-you for helping them get on the right road. Gaynah saw this as an insult and threw her candy in the bush.

"Do they think I've never seen candy?" she said in complete disgust. "My brother sends me American candy every month."

The new girl would be the second stranger to ever venture up Sycamore Hill in the last year. And no one can stop talking about it. If this is true and a girl really is coming here, then it could change our entire summer.

Nothing exciting ever happens here. Some of the adults pick fruits from the fields to sell, while some work out of town in the big hotels. A few, like Papa, go fishing early in the morning. If they catch anything, they sell it at the market in town. I used to go with him to catch an early surf. Now that I don't surf anymore, there's not much to do except laze around by the river and play a few games. Most days, though, this is what we do. Sit around waiting for something to happen.

That's why a new girl has us all so excited. Where is she from? Why is she here? Is she real or is she an alien? Gaynah said she saw an alien once down by Ms. Gee's guava tree. The alien had eight legs and three eyes and told her not to tell anyone because humans might hurt her. Of course, Gaynah being Gaynah, she told everyone she saw.

"Are you sure she's real, this girl?" I ask, pushing away the curly bangs I thought were a good idea this morning. Gaynah's big brown eyes widen with shock that I could ever question her. She flicks her long, straightened hair, which will have reverted to curly by the end of the day.

It's not that I don't believe there could be a new girl. It's just that Gaynah has a way of being in the middle of every drama on the hill. Usually the drama has already happened by the time she tells us, so we never actually get to witness it. The new girl could be real—chances are, she isn't—but it's summer and we have nothing else to do.

It would be nice to have someone new. Maybe this new girl will know some new games we can play, or have stories about where she came from. Maybe she will speak a different language or have a talent she can teach us. I get a little excited thinking of the possibilities.

It's midday, and the sun is at its hottest. It burns my dark brown skin as though someone is holding my arm over a fire. There is no shelter here like there is up at the house. On the roadside, the scorching heat has no pity on us.

I wipe sweat off my forehead and flick it onto the ground. Gaynah grimaces, as if the very sight of me disgusts her.

"She's not just any girl," she retorts in her usual snooty voice. She adjusts her little crossover bag that she proudly wears everywhere because her brother sent it from America. "I think she might be foreign."

I roll my eyes. Oh, she's foreign now. Next she'll be telling us the girl is another alien that she saw.

Out of the corner of my eye, I spot Calvin leaving his house, a surfboard under his arm. His short black curls shine in the sun, and glimmers of gold bounce off his skin.

Calvin uses his hand to protect his eyes from the sun

and calls to Anton, his tall, lanky friend whose father is a police officer. Anton strolls over and meets him, pushing his glasses up the bridge of his nose. As they approach, Calvin nods at me and says, "We're going for a surf. You coming?"

I lower my eyes to the ground and shake my head.

"Anton's brother is going to be there, if that's what you're worried about. You know my dad would never let me go without a chaperone."

I draw a face in the dirt with my finger so I don't have to look at him. "I said no." The truth is, the sea sounds perfect right now. My sweat feels like slime on my forehead, and my body is screaming for a breeze.

He walks off, shrugging. "I'm going to keep asking until you change your mind."

I feel Gaynah stiffen beside me. "But you'll miss the new girl." She pouts, because Gaynah thinks pouting gets her anything she wants. Calvin doesn't answer her. Maybe he doesn't hear, or maybe he does but doesn't care to meet the new girl.

"I'll tell him about the new girl at the game tomorrow," I say, feeling a little sorry for her. The game is "pick leaf," and all the kids on the hill play it every summer.

Gaynah snorts. "If you remember."

"Really?" I say through clenched teeth.

Mama tells me I must think before I have an outburst. "If you pause for five seconds, you will have a completely different reaction," she says. So I count as Gaynah fidgets with her bag and smooths the blue dress she is wearing.

One.

Two.

Three.

"Well, it's true. Everyone knows you don't remember anything."

That's not true. I remember some things. I remember when Gaynah is a good friend and when she is not. I remember what happened a few weeks ago, even last month. Even some things last year.

I remember that my name is Clara Dee-Henson, and I remember I am twelve years old. I know I live on a small island that tourists call exotic. I know I used to love surfing every morning while Papa went fishing, but I don't do that anymore. Something happened that made me forget everything that happened last summer.

Sometimes the memories come back to me in drips, like a tap that won't turn off no matter how hard I try. Sometimes Mama fills in the blanks. She'll say, "You spent the summer down at the river," or, "You went to the beach with Gaynah, do you remember?" She'll tell me small details, like what I was wearing, what time we left for the beach, how we had a nice snapper for dinner that Papa had caught on his fishing trip. Sometimes those memories stick so fast, I think they're mine, but they're not. They are hers.

Sometimes, like now, Gaynah uses my memory lapse to remind me that I'm not like everyone else. That I'm different. She frowns at me. "You're not going to cry, are you?"

"No."

Four.

Five.

She sighs, standing up, "You're such a baby, Clara. You cry about everything." She circles her finger beside her head.

I'm on my feet before I know it. "I am not crazy!" I scream. Everyone looks over at us, and the busy chatter stops. I try to think of something smart to say, something that will put her in her place, but nothing comes to mind, so I push her out of the way. I don't wait to see if she fell over and dirtied her pretty blue dress. Instead, I run up the hill before anyone can see the tears brimming in my eyes.

"Don't you want to see the girl with the bows in her hair?" she calls after me in a sickly-sweet voice that is meant to upset me even more.

"I don't care if her hair is on fire!" I scream, marching up the hill. "And your dress looks like it was made by an old lady."

Mama was wrong. Counting doesn't work.

CHAPTER
TWO

I HAVE A SECRET HIDEOUT BEHIND the house. A hole in the base of the hill that separates our house from the Wilson twins behind us. No one knows about this hole except me and Gaynah. We dug it out two summers ago so we'd have somewhere to hide when we stole the mangos off the ground. Papa always said we are not to touch the mangos unless they're bruised, but bruised mangos are not nice to look at, so we always steal a few and eat them in the dugout. Sometimes I come here by myself, like now. I sit cross-legged in the hole and bite into a ripe mango.

Gaynah will keep the new girl for herself anyway. There's no point in me being there. She will be the first to throw herself in front of her and appoint herself the hill leader. She will tell the new girl everything about everyone, including me. By tomorrow the new girl will know that Calvin is the popular boy who likes to surf. His father is Pastor Brown, who holds Saturday- and Sunday-morning church that goes on all day.

She will tell the new girl she has a crush on Calvin but Calvin never notices. She will say with her nose in the air that her mother is the head teacher of our school and has already secured a spot at the best university on the island for her. Even though she secretly thinks her mother is too controlling. She will tell the new girl about the Wilson twins, who are hardly ever home because they are relay champions and run for our parish. She will tell her about miserable Ms. Gee, who yells at everyone, and about our game of pick leaf tomorrow. But most of all, she will tell her about me. I will not get a chance to be Clara, another girl on the hill. By the time I see her, I will already be Clara, the girl who remembers nothing.

Mama is calling me, as she does every day when she leaves for town. "Clara, I'm going to the market. Are you coming?" Usually I hide in the dugout until she leaves. But today, the dugout doesn't seem to be far enough away from Gaynah. My thoughts flit from one answer to the other. I get ready to leave the dugout; then I change my mind. My heart feels as though it is going a hundred miles an hour, as if I am bracing myself to jump off a cliff.

I take a deep breath and climb out, running around the house just as Mama is about to disappear down the hill.

"Wait," I call.

She stops and turns, a box of fruit balanced on her head. Her long braids pulled into a high bun make a nook for the fruit. She looks back at me expectantly.

My chest rises and falls as I contemplate changing my mind. "You coming?" she asks, surprised.

I nod. "I need to get my board."

"Clara, I don't want you to . . ."

"I know, Mama." I sigh. I know what she's going to say. What she always says. *I don't want you to go in the water unless your father's there.* I don't know if she keeps saying it because she thinks I won't remember, like I don't remember what happened last summer. Or if she says it because that's what mamas do; they repeat things over and over to annoy you.

As we walk down the small hill from our house to the main road, I can see Gaynah is still waiting for her phantom girl. I balance the small foam board on my head, matching Mama's footsteps in the dirt as she carries mangos from our garden to sell at the market. She wears a simple black vest that hugs her full figure and a loose wrap skirt that flaps against her legs.

We pass Gaynah on the road. She checks her perfectly manicured nails, pretending she doesn't see me.

We continue along the narrow road that curves into Sycamore Hill and down a steep incline toward the village. There is nothing up here but the river, fields of trees, and our imaginations. Everyone knows each other on the hill, from Pastor Brown to Ms. Gee. Our parents grew up together, and so did their parents. You live and you die here. No one leaves and no one new comes in. Sometimes that's a good thing because you know everyone, and everyone knows you. Other times you get tired of seeing the same faces and want something new.

What I love most about living here is my best friend. Gaynah lives downhill from our house. She is two months older than me. Really, we are cousins because her mom and my mom are sisters. But even if we weren't cousins, we would still be best friends. We are opposites, which is probably why we don't get along sometimes. She likes dressing up, while I find matching a top with your bottoms one of the cruelest ways to make humans suffer. No one should have to endure that. Mama always grimaces when she sees what I am wearing, but Gaynah doesn't care about hurting my feelings—she tells me to go back inside and try again. "You can't wear leggings under a dress, Clara."

"Why not?"

"Because you look like a beach umbrella."

I don't care for clothes like Gaynah, but she cares about my clothes. She wants to do well at school not because she enjoys it, but because her mother wants her to. While I like school. I help Gaynah with schoolwork and she helps me to be cool.

But somewhere along the way, she got tired of helping me. She moved on, only hanging out with me when no one else was around. Even then, she always had something to say about what I was wearing, or saying, or not remembering. We argue; then we make up. That's how it's always been.

This time, though, we haven't made up. I don't know why, but she no longer wants to hang out with me, and when she does, she never has anything nice to say.

Mama glances behind her occasionally, I guess to make sure I haven't changed my mind and disappeared back up the hill. She flashes me an encouraging smile when she sees I am still here.

A hot ten-minute walk later, and the road opens into Sycamore Square. The noise, the people, the smell hit you all at once. Our town, known for its fishing, is called Sycamore. We have a supermarket, a police station, a courthouse, a small church, and a hospital.

We also have a movie theater, but Mr. Hammond only shows films he likes. Usually kung fu films starring an actor named Bruce Lee. Mr. Hammond can talk for a long time about Bruce Lee. Mama says if he sees you, he will trick you into thinking he has something important to say, but really, he just wants to talk about Bruce Lee.

It's hot down here. Hotter than on Sycamore Hill, where if we're lucky we get a slight breeze from the forest. Walking into Sycamore Square is like walking into an oven. A noisy oven with people calling to each other, stray dogs barking, and the constant beep of horns. The courthouse is framed against the blue sky, the white paint barely hiding the cracks from the storm two summers ago, when a telephone pole fell and hit the building.

In the distance, beyond the cars and minibuses, taxi drivers shout their destinations, competing for customers. Beyond them, sea air wafts over the seawall. It mixes with the heat and the bodies, the car exhaust and the smell of fish. My white T-shirt and blue overalls cling to my body.

I run to catch up with Mama as she navigates the traffic circle with cars speeding around the corner. We pass the courthouse, only to cross over again to the market. I try to blow air on my skin, but my breath is as warm as the heat and makes no difference.

I wipe the sweat off my skin. Mama turns as we approach the market. "If you don't see your father—"

"—don't go in the water." I groan, "Mama, I won't."

"I'll come and get you when I'm done," she says, planting a kiss on my forehead before disappearing into a crowd of people. I wipe her kiss away, afraid someone from school might have seen, then take the small gap between the wall that separates the market from the beach and walk down a narrow path. The path stops right on the sand, and that's where I stop too. My breath catches in my throat as I look out at the sea. Waves crash onto the white sand and I step back, as though they will reach me from here. I grip the board as my breathing gets quicker.

Calvin and Anton share the water with four or five out-of-town surfers. Tourists who travel around the world to surf. Occasionally there is a whoop as they catch a good wave. Anton's older brother, Junior, sits on the hot sand talking to a girl, his teeth perfectly white and his Afro fade newly cut. Occasionally he glances at the sea to check on Calvin and Anton. I'm surprised he gave up his time to watch them. Usually Junior is too busy with girls for his brother. But I guess things have changed.

I search the beach for Papa and spot him in the distance cleaning his boat. I shuffle along the sand until my back is against the wall, and that's where I stay until Calvin finds me. He must have spotted me when he came back in from riding the waves, even though I tried to stay hidden. He beckons me over. When I don't move, he drops his board in the sand and walks over.

"You're here," he says, looking down at me, water dripping from the curls in his hair. He observes me for a second, then sits next to me. I feel so stupid that I came down here thinking everything would be okay. Now Calvin will know how scared I am. He will tell Gaynah, and she will use it against me like she does everything else.

"Pick leaf tomorrow," he says, resting his elbows on his knees. He grins at me. "You ready to lose?"

I scoff, rolling my eyes. "Not this year. We have a plan that is going to annihilate you all."

He laughs, "Big word. Let's see if you remember it tomorrow when you lose."

CHAPTER
THREE

THE GAME PICK LEAF HAS THREE rules.

1. You can only pick a leaf from the tree named by the appointed leader.
2. The leaf must come from the tree itself and not the ground.
3. Never, ever, steal the leaf from your opponent. That is an automatic disqualification for your entire team.

The leader, usually Calvin or one of his friends, chooses the name of the tree. The first one to pick a leaf from that tree and bring it back to the starting point is the winner of that round.

The game always starts from my front yard. Maybe because our house is at a point higher than the others, making the race back to the finish more exciting. We push and shove our competition out of the way, even going as far as to step over them if it gets us ahead.

Or maybe it's because our house is surrounded by the most trees: A guinep tree hanging over Uncle Albert's house below. At the back of the house a mango tree, and a banana grove down a steep embankment.

Eldorath is the only other person with a garden filled with trees. He is the only one around here who lives in a big house too. But it's too far up on the hill for any of us. It used to be a plantation house, when the British owned our island. Eldorath is family, but you would never know it. He doesn't come to our house every night like the rest of the village. He doesn't come around at Christmas or birthdays. In fact, we hardly ever see Eldorath. Not anymore. Not since the town turned against him.

He doesn't have the most popular tree, though. He doesn't have a guava tree.

If the call is for a guava leaf, you have to trek down the hill, along the dirt road past Pastor Brown's house. Then left, down a steep embankment to where Ms. Gee lives, behind a forest of trees.

Ms. Gee is blind in one eye and nearly blind in the

other. Mama says she might be the most miserable person she knows.

There is a joke around the hill that if you need a knife, you can ask Ms. Gee, because her tongue can cut anything. Ms. Gee doesn't leave her house unless it's life-or-death. All she does is sit on her veranda in her rocking chair screaming some poor kid's name to help her with her chores. She doesn't pick on anyone in particular; we've all had our turn cleaning Ms. Gee's yard or washing her clothes.

But she has the one thing we all want: the guava tree. The one tree that sends us all into a panic. No one wants to enter Ms. Gee's yard for the guava leaf. There is one other guava tree in the village. It's a ten-minute trek down the hill, outside the school. Most of the kids will go for that tree, but not me and Gaynah. We know that Ms. Gee's tree is worth the risk, if we do it properly. Going into Ms. Gee's yard means extra points for sheer bravery. But also, her house is closer. If we can creep into Ms. Gee's yard without her knowing, we can be back with a leaf before the other kids have even reached the school. An easy win for us.

Amber Wilson, the taller of the twins, and the bossier of the two, picks the teams today. She splits us into groups, she and her sister in one, Anton and Calvin in the other, which leaves me with Gaynah. Amber gives me a "sorry, not sorry" shrug. Calvin offers me the look of pity that I see in everyone's eyes these days.

"Want me to be on your team?" he asks. Anton isn't happy with this and pulls Calvin back.

"No," I say, folding my arms firmly against my chest. I can hear Gaynah huffing to my left. She turns her head away, nose in the air, as though she doesn't care that Calvin invited himself onto my team. But she cares.

I don't want Calvin on my team anyway. He is my main competition, and I already told him I was going to beat him.

It was always meant to be me and Gaynah against them. It's one of the few times Gaynah has agreed with me that we can't let the other teams win. But we haven't spoken since yesterday. I'm still mad at her for calling me a baby, and she's obviously mad too, because her lips are pursed tightly together and she refuses to even look at me.

When it comes time to find out the tree we are picking from, of course Amber chooses the guava tree. It's the one that causes the most chaos, and the one she and her sister are most certain they will win.

Gaynah and I may not be friends, but she needs me to help her get the leaf. A win for her means status among the other groups, and status means the attention of Calvin Brown.

I don't care for any of their friendships. All I want is to prove that Gaynah can't do any of this without me. She needs me.

We follow the others down the hill. Each group splits in different directions with excited squeals. Gaynah stands in the middle of the road, the only road that leads up and down this hill. She watches the others leave in the forlorn way you see dogs do when their owner leaves them. I find a rock and sit down. I'm not kissing her feet. If she wants to play, she's going to have to speak to me.

I find a stick and draw in the dirt because, let's be honest, I can stay silent for hours. Days, even. Gaynah, on the other hand—

"Fine," she huffs, "come on." She marches off shouting her plan, which isn't her plan at all; it's ours. We spent hours planning our attack.

"You distract Ms. Gee, and I'll run to the tree and pick the leaf."

That is not the plan.

"Why don't *you* distract Ms. Gee?" I say, thinking I've had my fair share of that miserable old woman.

"Because you won't remember the plan," she retorts. "We'll get caught."

I don't know what she means. I don't forget things *now*; I forget things that happened before. I remember she was mean to me yesterday. It's Gaynah who messes things up.

She's clumsy, she's not fast, and she's terrible at jumping. But I think this has nothing to do with the game. I think Gaynah is just trying to hurt me by reminding me I have problems with my brain.

"I get caught because you always make me go," I reply angrily.

"How would you know? You don't remember."

"I remember everything that happened yesterday and last week and last month."

She faces me head-on, hands on hips. "Do you really not remember what happened last summer, Clara, or are you pretending for attention?"

Tears brim in my eyes and I'm so mad at myself for crying. My lips twitch. "Why would I make that up?"

She waves me away in the same superior manner her mother does. I hate it when she does that. I want to tell her not to talk to me that way. But instead I am forced to catch my breath as pictures of the sea flash through my mind. My legs become unsteady and I look for something to hold on to, but there is nothing.

Without looking back, Gaynah marches off, her walking swiftly turning into a run as she tries to beat me to the house.

She only has a few seconds on me, so despite my shortness of breath, I chase her at full speed, ignoring the sharp stones digging into my feet. I charge up the embankment, where the soft grass cushions my soles.

As I gain on her, she pushes faster. Her thighs bouncing off each other, her long hair blowing wildly.

Out of the two of us, I am the faster runner. I came in second in the class race and fifth in the entire school. Gaynah didn't place in either of them.

Ahead, the embankment comes to a sudden end and rejoins the dirt track. If I run fast enough, I can jump ahead of her and win. We are neck and neck; I can hear her heaving for breath and I know she is struggling. Without breaking a sweat, I dig my head into my chest and power past her with ease.

Clara: 1.

Gaynah: 0.

By the time she reaches me, I am already leaning against the coconut tree, arms folded, legs crossed. Usually we would fall on the ground laughing, but this time a slight smirk plants on my face.

She slows down to a casual walk before reaching me, her head stuck in the air, her heavy breathing giving her away.

Without a word, she strides past me and up the dugout path to Ms. Gee's house. I follow, but the victory turns sour in my mouth because I miss my best friend.

CHAPTER
FOUR

MS. GEE'S WOODEN HOUSE BALANCES ON four stilts. It looms before us like a beast daring us to trespass. Its red zinc roof and red steps that lead up to the veranda are the only spots of color on the otherwise gloomy house. It's unlike most of the other houses around here because she refused to replace it with brick to make it safer. Storms are a regular occurrence on the island, one of the drawbacks of living somewhere tropical. I have been through two storms and one hurricane. Each time it comes, Sycamore feels it. Our houses get damaged, Papa's boat needs fixing for the hundredth time, trees fall, the roads flood, and if you're lucky, school is out. Mama says Ms. Gee just doesn't like being told what to do, even if you're trying to help her.

Gaynah lowers herself behind the tall grass. I creep up behind her. We peer through the grass stems, toward the veranda. The rocking chair creaks with every move.

The back of Ms. Gee's unmistakable gray bun is the only thing we can see of her. Gaynah gives me the thumbs-up.

I swallow hard and straighten my frame from the cramped position I'm folded into. Forcing one foot in front of the other, my eyes fixed on the back of Ms. Gee's head, I step into the yard. That's when I see her. The new girl. She is sitting on the veranda wall, reading a book and wearing an oversized multicolored top over jean shorts, her curly black hair pulled high into two buns finished off with two giant white bows. Just like Gaynah said. Our eyes meet and I stop short.

She is a rainbow of colors exploding into Ms. Gee's gloomy house. She stares at me and I stare at her and neither of us moves. Out of the corner of my eye, I see Gaynah creeping on all fours toward the tree. She freezes too when she sees the girl. A look of horror explodes over Gaynah's face. She has been caught creeping into Ms. Gee's yard, and Gaynah doesn't like being in trouble. Neither do I, but I won't get punished the way she will. Her mother won't let her see daylight for at least a week.

The girl's eyes screw up tight, and her jaw moves from side to side. Gaynah and I sneak a look at the tree. I know she is thinking what I'm thinking: Should we just run for it? Time is ticking, and Calvin and his group are surely on their way back now.

As if she senses an intruder, Ms. Gee's head twitches to the side, and she leans forward.

Nobody moves. Not even the girl.

The rocking comes to a screeching halt, and Ms. Gee lurches forward. Her nose jerks upward, and she sniffs the air like an animal trying to catch the scent of its prey.

Without warning, as if spooked by something, Gaynah jumps to her feet and runs across the yard toward the guava tree, kicking stones into the air as she goes. Quickly, to mask the noise, I purposely walk into the pan that collects rainwater for when the water gets cut off, which happens at least once a month.

The sound of my feet in the water pan is hollow, but it is enough to have Ms. Gee jumping out of her chair. She grabs her stick and scurries to the railing

"Who's there?"

Gaynah freezes inches away from the tree.

"Who's there? Are you trying to trick a blind woman? Wait until I tell your parents."

That is a threat I know Gaynah does not take lightly. I see her legs shake at the mere mention of her parents. The snotty girl disappears and is replaced by the girl I know so well. The girl scared of never being good enough for her mother.

"It's me, Ms. Gee." I run around the veranda to the front and stand at the bottom of the steps. Ms. Gee's frown deepens. She cocks her head to the side.

"Clara?"

"Yes, ma'am."

She leans over the veranda railing and tilts her head again, then straightens and looks directly at me.

"Anybody else in my tree?"

I shrug while motioning to Gaynah to do it now.

"Clara? Child, are you deaf?"

"It's only me, Ms. Gee," I say.

She shuffles along the railing. Using her stick, she hurries down the wooden steps until she reaches the yard. I want to scream *Abort! Abort!* but Gaynah is too focused on the leaf to pay me any attention.

Gaynah makes a final lunge at the branch and catches the edge of a leaf. She curls her fingers around the stem and yanks at it. The leaf slips through her fingers, and it splits, so all that's left in her hand is just a small piece of guava leaf, but for her it is enough. She turns on her heels and disappears down the gully.

I watch her go, wondering if she will hand the leaf in, then come back to share the blame.

But I have a sinking feeling she won't be back. Before, when we got caught, we got caught together. She would not leave my side, and I would not leave hers.

"Clara?"

I turn to Ms. Gee, who is glaring above my head with such intense rage, I think she might self-combust.

"Yes, ma'am."

"Get in the house now."

"Yes, ma'am."

These days, I face Ms. Gee alone.

CHAPTER
FIVE

THE SUN SINKS INTO THE HORIZON, welcoming another cool evening breeze. The night air fills with loud music and laughter from our house.

It feels so lonely down here in Ms. Gee's house, wrapped in the quiet but still able to hear people in the distance.

As I finish ironing the last of her clothes and begin to fold them, the new girl bursts into Ms. Gee's bedroom like a firework. "Hi, I'm Rudy. What's your name?" She has a strong New York accent. Her face is round like a dough ball and her skin is a dark reddish brown like the sun as it sets in the nighttime. She plonks herself onto the bed with a smile as wide as the room.

"Clara," I say as steady as possible. My heart is beating

fast and I don't know why. I feel her eyes on me and wait for the questions—what were we doing in Ms. Gee's yard, what kind of person sneaks onto someone's land just to get a leaf. I can imagine how bad it must have looked.

I turn my back on her to place Ms. Gee's flowery skirts in the second drawer from the bottom.

"So, what were you doing?"

I place the skirts neatly in the drawer. "When?" I don't look at her because for some reason I feel guilty, and Ms. Gee must be close to her, so maybe she's mad at me.

"Before, when you were creeping around the house."

I swallow hard. She's only been here one day. She knows nothing about us or our game. I press the skirts down so they fit in the drawer while counting under my breath.

I can't afford to lose my temper in Ms. Gee's house. If she hears me, she'll find something else for me to do, and I could be here all night.

"I wasn't creeping," I say as calmly as I can.

The girl spread-eagles on Ms. Gee's bed, staring up at the zinc roof. "My mother says if you're creeping, you're not doing anything good."

This girl has lost her mind. I mean, who does she think she is! I don't even know her, and she thinks she knows me.

Count, Clara. Count.

"Well, maybe your mother was only talking about

you," I snap. "Creeping seems to be *your* thing." My voice is loud and crackly. My chest is rising and falling fast, and I'm pointing at her like Mama waves her finger at me when I've done something that disappoints her. The girl turns her head to look at me, completely unfazed by my outburst.

"I didn't mean to upset you." She sits up and dangles her feet off the bed. "I only wondered what you were doing, that's all." She walks around the bed and heads for the door. I listen to the door close and her bare feet skip across the pinewood floor.

I hurriedly finish my chores and rush by a woman in Ms. Gee's kitchen. She smiles when she sees me, and I assume it's the American girl's mother because they look the same, except her hair is short and dyed red. Her face lights up when she smiles, and her teeth are almost as white as Pastor Brown's.

I find Ms. Gee in the same place I left her, on the veranda. I don't bother to ask if she wants to come to dinner because I know what she will say. *Do you think I can't cook for myself? I don't need your charity or your mother's poisonous food.*

Instead, I wait impatiently as she reels off the chores on her list one by one, demanding to know if I have completed them just the way she has asked. I don't know why she needs me. She has a live-in maid for the summer. I cast a fiery look over at Rudy, who is sitting on the veranda wall again with the same book.

"Can I go now, Ms. Gee?"

She responds with the folding of her arms, leaning back into her chair, and staring into the night sky.

As I walk down the steps, the American lady comes out onto Ms. Gee's porch and asks if I want her to walk me home.

Ms. Gee scoffs before I can answer. "Walk her home? She's got two feet, hasn't she?"

"Clara, is it?" the woman asks, ignoring Ms. Gee, and I think she must have heard me talking to her daughter. I flush, realizing that she might have heard everything I said.

I nod.

"It's pretty dark out there, Clara. Do you normally walk home by yourself?"

I look from the woman to the girl to Ms. Gee.

"Yes, I walk home by myself," I tell her, and I am aware how different my accent is from hers.

"By yourself?" she repeats, her eyes wide, as if I just told her I have no mama and papa.

"Yes, by herself," Ms. Gee snaps. "She's been walking round here since she learned how. What do you think we're going to do to her?"

The woman's face tightens, and she folds her arms across her chest just like Ms. Gee does after she explodes.

"I'm not saying that, Mom, but in New York . . ."

Now it's my eyes that are wide. Ms. Gee is her mother? I can't hide the shock as they argue back and forth. I didn't know Ms. Gee had a daughter. I try to memorize their conversation so I can tell Gaynah when I see her. She loves talking about other people's business.

"Yes, yes. This isn't New York. This is Sycamore, and there isn't a soul on this hill that would harm that girl. You used to go off by yourself too. You would remember that if you hadn't gone gallivanting to America." Ms. Gee shoos me away as if I were a hen trying to climb her stairs for crumbs. "Go on, go."

I hesitate as the woman begins to say something else, then changes her mind and returns into the house, slamming the door behind her.

It is a dark walk back from Ms. Gee's house. The only light comes from the half-moon hovering above me as a guide. My feet sink into familiar ditches as I skillfully maneuver over the ground, climbing the embankment, then jumping over the same nest of stones that dug into my feet this afternoon.

I can't stop thinking about Ms. Gee having a daughter. I wonder why she's never mentioned her. They don't seem to like each other much, but that's no surprise; no one likes Ms. Gee much. And the new girl isn't the person I thought she would be. Turns out she's just an annoying girl wearing too many colors and with too much to say. She and Gaynah will have plenty in common.

The screech of crickets in the trees above can be heard between the outbursts of laughter coming from home. As I climb the hill to our house, I see people filling our veranda and spilling out onto the yard. Our house is like this every night. It becomes a meeting place for people when the sun goes down. Papa is handing out drinks and sharing a joke with Gaynah's father. Papa's tall, thin figure makes a shadow on the wall of the house, and his twisted hair falls just below his ears. Mama can never get him to sit down long enough to do those twists, so sometimes she'll do it while he is sleeping.

I walk along the perimeter of the yard to avoid detection. I'm not in the mood for people today. With Gaynah leaving me at Ms. Gee's, Ms. Gee forcing me to do her chores, and that horrible American girl gloating because she thinks she knows everything, the last thing I want is to be around people.

I spot Gaynah sitting on the veranda wall next to Calvin. So she doesn't care where I've been. I feel the sting at the back of my throat, and my eyes well up. Well, now she won't get to know what I know, that Ms. Gee has a daughter and they hate each other. I rush around the side of the house and into the darkness, where I won't be seen.

I hide in the dugout with a few bruised mangos Mama left on the ground. I used to take my surfboard down to the beach with Papa. It was the only place I could go and forget everything. When I was on my board waiting for that swell, it was as if there were no one else in this world but me.

It was Papa who introduced us all to surfing. Me, Calvin, Anton. He fell in love with it when he worked as a lifeguard. No one in Sycamore surfed until Papa brought tourists to the swell where he lived. He also brought a new love of the sea with him. After his father died, he said it took him some time to want to be near water. Before last summer, before everything changed, we would spend time on the beach, just me and him, and he would tell me how being a lifeguard helped him to understand the sea, and how surfing made him fall in love with it again.

It was New Year's Day when he gave me my first lesson. The tradition was for all of Sycamore Hill to go to the beach. The adults were setting out food and we kids were playing tag in the sand when Mama came over and told me Ms. Gee wanted someone to help her back at the house. Ms. Gee didn't have a phone, so she would just yell until someone heard her. Pastor Brown told her he would send someone, and that someone was me. Papa was just about to go out into the water, and he asked if I wanted to come to get away from Ms. Gee. I had watched him many times in awe as he skimmed the waves with his board, so I was breathless with excitement when he said he would teach me even as Mama yelled at him to stop overruling her.

"It's the holidays," he said to Mama. "Ms. Gee can do without her for one day."

"Can you teach me too?" Calvin asked. Papa glanced over at Mama, who sighed, shaking her head.

"You can explain it to Ms. Gee when we get home," she said, walking away.

Papa raised his eyebrows at us mischievously. "Okay, one at a time," he said, and that was it. I was hooked.

I think that's when things changed between me and Gaynah. I don't think she wanted me to spend any time with Calvin.

CHAPTER
SIX

"CLARA, CAN YOU DO SOMETHING OTHER than be under my feet all day?" Mama whips the broom over my feet.

"I don't have anywhere to go," I mumble, holding my legs up in the air so she can clean the veranda. Mama stands up straight, her hands on her hips, her braids hidden under a silk scarf. She frowns at me, and her thick brows meet in the middle of her forehead. "Nowhere to go? The sun is out, and it's summer break. Find something to do." She nudges me with the broom, but I don't budge. She sighs, swishing the brush across the floor. "Go to the river. You might find someone down there."

I roll my eyes when her back is turned. Gaynah will be down by the river, and I will never speak to her again as long as I live. I would rather put myself in a hole in the ground for fifteen years with no food and no water. No, I would rather be thrown in the very deep end of the sea, where the sharks live, with no life jacket, than speak to Gaynah again. And that's saying something, because I don't like sharks. Or water.

"Clara!"

I snap out of my daydream. Mama is not amused.

"Go to the river, now."

"I don't want to."

She takes a breath. "You can't keep running away from things that scare you," she says gently, and now she's looking at me with sadness in her eyes. I don't think she's talking about Gaynah anymore.

"And make sure you tell Albert where you're going so he can keep an eye on you."

I groan. That's all I need, Uncle Albert's beady eyes spying on me. I drag my feet across the veranda and down the cracked steps that no one seems to want to fix.

My home is rugged and flawed. It sits on the hill overlooking the ocean, half-brick, half-wood, painted sky blue. It used to be white stone and brown wood, but today Papa is painting it blue to match the sky.

I climb down the embankment that leads into the banana grove behind the house. The leaves hover over my head like giant umbrellas, and it's a nice shade from the sun. I see Uncle Albert in the distance cutting down bananas to take into town, and he waves, then wipes sweat from his forehead.

"You going to the river?" he calls. I nod and he gives me a thumbs-up.

The ground goes flat where Uncle Albert works. Then it slopes steeply toward the river.

My plan is to sit on the hill between the trees, but I hear loud laughter and Gaynah's screeching voice. I pause, looking back up the hill.

I continue downward, still hidden, and sit with my back against a tree trunk, digging the heels of my shoes into the dirt to stop me from sliding. I'll sit here for a little while. Maybe I will go farther down and maybe I won't, but I am here, and that's all Mama asked of me.

I watch between the trees as Gaynah, Calvin, Anton, and the Wilson twins sit at the edge of the river, dipping their feet in. Anton cups his hands under the water, and everyone except Gaynah scrambles to their feet to get away from him. No one would dare get Gaynah wet when she's wearing her favorite bag. They would never hear the end of it.

Anton chases them with a small pool in his hand that quickly slips between his fingers until he is left with nothing but wet hands. He chases Amara Wilson, the elder twin by three minutes and the more fun of the two. She wears her hair the same way every day, just like her sister, in lots of short braids. It never changes, even when they're competing in a relay race.

Anton tries to wipe his wet hands on her face. She squeals, running away from him. I can't help but feel a pang of jealousy watching. Amara starts to climb the hill to get away, when she sees me.

Anton catches up with her and follows her stare until he also sees me hiding in the trees. He breaks into a wide grin and waves. Slowly I raise my hand and wave back hesitantly. Anton and I don't really talk. He tolerates me for Calvin's sake, but I can tell he would prefer it if Calvin didn't keep inviting me to join them.

"Hey, hole girl," he calls. "Why are you not in your hole today?" His smile turns into a laugh and he retreats back down the hill.

I pull my hand down and hide it in my lap. How did he know? I feel the rush of panic as I try to think about all the people who knew about our hideout. No one knew. No one but me and Gaynah.

She told them. Gaynah told them about our secret place. How could she! That was our secret.

I will not cry.

One.

Two.

My eyes meet Gaynah's, and she's smiling too. I clamber to my feet and run up the hill.

I will not cry.

Three.

Four.

"Hey! Careful!"

I look up and it's her, the American girl. She's wearing a purple swimsuit with a pleated white skirt. Her hair is out of its buns today, and it's a mass of tight curls held down by a headband made of pink and white flowers. I'm so shocked to see her that I forget to give her a cutting remark. She's wearing cat's-eye sunglasses again, so I can't see her eyes, but she's smiling like we are friends, and we are not friends.

"Hello, Clara, are you leaving already?" she asks, surprised, but I think it might be fake surprise. Like she's trying to be smart or something.

"I was just passing through," I say in a strange high-pitched voice. I sound like those posh ladies from East Avenue with the big houses. I continue up the hill.

"But your friends are here."

See? Trying to be smart. Told you.

"They're not my friends," I shout. Loud enough for everyone to hear. Everyone. "You can have them."

My heart is beating fast as I picture Gaynah's face. She will pretend she doesn't care. She might even pretend she hasn't heard me.

But she heard me. I made sure of it.

"I'll be here tomorrow if you change your mind," Rudy shouts back.

I reach the top of the hill and turn to look down the slope. Rudy places her towel on a rock and wades into the river. She doesn't seem to notice Gaynah laughing and pointing at her.

I try to count but I can't focus, I'm so mad.

One.

Two.

Three.

I don't know what I am angrier about: Gaynah telling Calvin and his friends about our secret hideout or Gaynah laughing at Rudy.

I decide I am angrier about the hideout. That was our secret, where we went to get away from everything. Her bossy mom, her quiet father, who always has somewhere to go but no one knows where. My mom nagging at me to do things, and Papa . . . sometimes I even need to get away from Papa.

I storm through the banana grove, ignoring Uncle Albert calling me. I don't even know how Gaynah and I became friends. How did someone so mean become my friend? Did I get knocked on the head? Or did I just forget what kind of friend she was?

Before I know it, I am at the house. Mama calls me as I pass her on the veranda, but her voice is distant and morphs into Gaynah's laugh. All I can hear is her laughing. Her stupid, whiny laugh. She sounds like a tree frog.

In my bedroom, I drop to my knees and feel around for the memory box that holds stories of our friendship—things we would only talk about in our dugout. The silver pin we found in the river. The notes we would write each other in class. The blue top we both got when we begged our parents for it because we had seen it on our favorite celebrity in one of the magazines Gaynah's brother had sent her. The diary we shared, which no one else has seen. I grab it all under my arm and make my way out of the house.

"Clara, what is the matter with you?"

Mama won't understand. She'll tell me Gaynah didn't mean it. *It's just Gaynah. Why do you let her get to you?* she'll say. I don't want to hear that right now. I head back down the hill, through the banana grove and through the trees, almost falling down the embankment to the river. Rudy is still there, making two sticks dance on the water. The group is on the other side of the river, watching her like she's a TV show.

I stand at the edge of the river, throw off the lid of the memory box, and dump it into the water. The blue top, the diary, the letters, all of it. If Gaynah wants to be spiteful, then I can be spiteful too.

My heart is beating so fast, I can barely catch my breath. Staring Gaynah dead in the eye, I bang the bottom of the box just to make sure it's empty. Then I turn on my heels and retrace my steps home for the second time that day.

CHAPTER
SEVEN

AFTER THE INCIDENT AT THE RIVER, I realize there is no one I can trust. So I spend the rest of the day under the mango tree cleaning my board. I haven't surfed since last summer, but I make sure to clean it and check for any damage almost every day.

The first few times I surfed, Papa lent me his board, which had been given to him by a tourist when he worked at the resort. He loved that surfboard and would never leave me alone with it in case I damaged it.

One Christmas, Papa asked Clinton, Gaynah's father, to make me a surfboard of my own. He had never made one before, but he was a carpenter, so he was used to making things. When Papa gave it to me, he told me if I damaged it, I wouldn't be getting another one, so I keep it in my room out of the sun, checking it for dust every day.

I can hear Mama talking to someone around the front of the house. I can't hear what they're saying, but I know it's not Papa. I pick myself up from the dirt and walk to the wall of the house to try to listen. Their words are muffled, but I bet it's Gaynah telling on me. I peek around the wall. It's Gaynah and Calvin standing behind Uncle Albert. He is handing the memory box back to Mama.

I step back out of sight, my heart beating fast. Gaynah and Calvin told Uncle Albert about the box. Why? Are they trying to get me in trouble?

"Clara!" Mama calls, and it's that voice again. The strained, painful voice that so often sits like a wall between us.

My heart sinks.

I use the back door to enter the house, walk through the living room, and emerge at the front door. Mama spins around to look at me in complete bewilderment. She holds my blue top, which is dripping wet. "Why, Clara?" she asks, and I can't tell if she wants to hold me or scold me.

I lower my eyes to the ground. It seemed to make so much sense when I did it. Prove to Gaynah I no longer cared about our memories. But seeing Mama upset makes me feel silly.

"I don't want it anymore," I mumble.

"But this isn't yours to throw away. There are things in here that don't belong to just you. Why did you do it?"

Because she makes fun of me. Because she makes fun of other people. Because she told everyone about our secret hideout.

"Clara."

I glance at Gaynah through misty eyes, but she won't look at me.

"Well, I'll get going, then," Uncle Albert says, and he flashes me a weak smile. Mama waits for them to leave before she closes the box. As she walks by me, she stops and rests her hand on my cheek. It's warm and a little wet from holding the dripping blue top. She stays only for a second before her arm drops and she disappears inside the house.

I've never heard Mama and Papa argue. Not really argue. I've heard them disagree on what TV show to watch, and heard Papa try to convince Mama to go fishing with him just once. Sometimes I hear them whispering about me. How they don't know what to do with me—Papa will say I need time and Mama will ask him how much more time.

I've never heard them argue like this.

I listen through the walls of my room. It is supposed to be Mama's birthday party tonight. Most of the hill, including Ms. Gee, is due in less than an hour, but I think I might have ruined it.

"She threw it all in the river. Look!"

"She's going through some stuff," Papa says, and I can imagine him trying to hug her, but she will push him away like she always does when she is mad.

"How much longer?" Mama says. "How much longer until we do something different, Lloyd?"

I don't know what she means by "do something different." What is it they want to do to me? Send me away? Where would they send me? I feel sick thinking about it.

Everything goes quiet after that. Maybe she allowed Papa to hold her; maybe she gave up and left the room. All I know is I can't bear to think I caused them this much pain.

Mama has created quite a setup for her own party. She doesn't allow anyone to plan anything for her because she always ends up redoing it the way she likes it. There are fairy lights all around the veranda. In one corner is a long table filled with every food imaginable. Curried chicken, curried lamb, fried fish, peppered prawns, dumplings, pumpkin, potato, rice and peas, and my favorite: carrot cake.

Papa turns on the sound system, and I help him with

the balloons while Mama finishes getting ready. We don't talk about the memory box, or how Mama is sad because of me. Instead, he hums along to the song playing, the bass making the entire house vibrate.

One by one, people begin to appear. The older neighbors turn up first; they are on time for everything. Everyone else will come at least a few hours into the party.

An hour later Calvin arrives with his mother and father. We exchange an awkward hello, and he follows his father over to the food. Ms. Gee arrives, her arm linked with Rudy's, Rudy's mother walking a step behind. I can't help but smile at what Rudy is wearing. The oversized blue bow in her hair matches her tights, which have small bows all over them. She covers the tights with a dress and black army boots. She hugs me tightly. I am finding it hard not to like Rudy.

Papa tries to help Ms. Gee into a chair, but Ms. Gee waves him away, saying she can sit down by herself, she's not an invalid.

Rudy links arms with me whether I want her to or not. We leave the veranda and step into the front yard. "What a view," she sighs, looking out to the city. Dots of yellow lights fill the horizon like flashlights. "You're so lucky, Clara."

"I guess," I say, but I'm distracted by Gaynah approaching the foot of the hill with her mother and father. They pass us without saying a word, but the cold glares from both Gaynah and her mother tell me how they really feel.

As if sensing the tension, Papa turns up the music, and the bass fills the entire yard, and probably the hill too. Papa rocks Mama from side to side, his head nestled into her neck until she has no option but to smile.

Rudy lets go of my arm. "Oh, I love dancing. It's one of my favorite things to do, as well as singing, acting, and playing the piano." She runs into the middle of the yard and spins round and round. She calls me over. "Clara, come on!" I'm not much of a public dancer. Especially not in front of Gaynah and her mother.

Calvin doesn't seem to mind the attention, though, because he joins her in the yard, copying Rudy and laughing at the funny faces she makes. I look up to see Gaynah seething. I try to hide a satisfied grin but fail miserably. As if sensing that her daughter is being outshone, Juliette turns to Mama and says something, her arms flying in the air. Mama starts to argue with her, and the mood changes again. Someone switches the music off just as Juliette shouts, "It's embarrassing. Look at her, acting as if nothing's wrong." Papa tells her to calm down, but this only makes her worse.

"Did you hear what she did at the river?" She's pointing

directly at me. "How long are we going to allow this disruptive behavior to go on? Aren't you embarrassed?"

"No," Mama and Papa say firmly.

"Whatever she's done," Ms. Gee chimes in, speaking to Juliette, "is it worth embarrassing the child like this?"

I think I might love Ms. Gee.

Juliette dismisses her with a roll of her eyes. "You don't know anything about it, so stay out of it."

"I know more than you think I do," Ms. Gee says, sitting so far at the edge of her chair, she is almost out of it. "I know we have bigger problems to fix in this town than some child upsetting you."

Juliette glares at Mama and Papa, but they fold their arms defiantly.

"Are you going to let her talk to me this way?"

Ms. Gee opens her mouth to reply, but Rudy's mom lays a firm hand on her knee. For once Ms. Gee complies and slides back in her seat. Which is not like Ms. Gee at all. I feel Rudy's hand slip into mine as Pastor Brown steps in between them. "Let us all calm down," he says, looking from Juliette to Ms. Gee. Everyone collectively lets out a sigh of relief that Pastor Brown has spoken. He puffs out his chest and scans the room the way he does when he is about to start a sermon.

Pastor Brown doesn't look like any of us on the hill. He

is smaller than any of the men here, and he is broad like he works out, but I've never even seen him run. His hair is short and wavy like Calvin's, and his teeth are so white, I once shut off the lights and pretended the electricity had gone out in church so we could see if his teeth were still shining.

Papa says people listen to him because he's the head of the church and he speaks for God, but I think it's because he looks like a movie star and people always listen to movie stars. Even when they're not saying anything worth listening to.

Everyone is quiet as he speaks to Mama. "For the sake of salvaging your evening, Alysa, maybe you can tell us how Clara was punished for the box."

He doesn't fool me, though. I know exactly what he is. A fraud. He is the one who turned the town against my uncle. He was the one who called my uncle the witch doctor, and the name stuck. Maybe that's why we don't get along. Maybe that's why he always adds my name in the church prayer. And tells Mama and Papa to encourage me to attend more Bible classes. Because he knows that I am not fooled by him.

Mama looks at Papa, and I can't believe she is even considering answering him. "Your daughter should have taken a few examples from mine," Juliette says with her chin in the air, the black freckles on her cheeks the only thing we have in common. "Then we might not be in this mess." I see Mama's face harden, and it is enough to make me move.

I push by Rudy, past Juliette, and inside the house. I find the memory box in my parents' room. On the dresser. Next to a photo of Nana and me sitting under the mango tree. The blue top is gone, and so are the mirror and the pin. But the diary is still there.

I hover over the box.

Count, Clara, count.

I place my hands firmly on my hips and stare hard at Nana's photo, willing it to calm me down. I close my eyes.

One, two, three, four.

Maybe Mama kept the box hoping I would change my mind and want it back. She's wrong. I don't want it back, but I'm glad she kept it.

One, two, three, four, five.

I breathe heavy through my nose, my chest rising and falling.

Four, five, six, seven.

I don't want to be mad, but all I can see is Juliette's sneer and all I can hear is her evil voice taunting me. Then Pastor Brown's growly voice telling Mama and Papa I need to be punished. I grab the diary and return to the veranda as Papa tries calming everyone down.

I flick the diary open under the glare of the veranda light, my chest pumping fast. I don't need to read the pages. I know every page by heart.

"Gaynah Campbell cheated on the math test when she was nine because she didn't know her eight times table. Gaynah doesn't like it when you make her corned beef sandwiches; she gives them to the dog outside school and tells you a bully from the high school stole them, but she can never remember his name because HE DOESN'T EXIST. Gaynah has a crush on Calvin Brown and that's the only reason she begged you to let her have private Bible study at Pastor Brown's house. Gaynah Campbell wishes her mother didn't teach at our school because she is embarrassed by the old granny clothes she wears." I catch my breath. Everyone is staring at me in horror. Juliette's mouth twists from side to side like a snake slithering toward you before it opens its jaw to swallow you whole. Mama has that look again. The one of desperation.

"Clara" is all she manages.

Pastor Brown demands that Mama and Papa punish me. "This is abhorrent behavior. You are members of this community. This"—he wags his finger at me—"this is inexcusable."

I want Mama to tell him that I was right to do what I did. That she will not quiet me, because I am just like her, like a force of wind that will not be tamed. Maybe that is the problem. I am too much like her, and I am not enough like them.

The diary falls out of my hands. I run down the steps and around the back. As I stumble down the hill, I hear Rudy shouting after me. And both our mamas yelling at us to come back.

CHAPTER
EIGHT

"WHO DOES SHE THINK SHE IS? She's not perfect. None of them are." I march ahead as Rudy tries to keep up with me. "I could have told her all the things her perfect daughter did to me, but I didn't."

"You sure showed them," Rudy says.

"That woman is the meanest person I've ever met. I thought it was Ms. Gee, but it's not."

"Grandma really came through for you," Rudy agrees.

I ignore her ongoing commentary and continue my rant.

"I'll bet she's in this mean-old-lady club, but she kicked everyone out for not being mean enough, because she's the meanest out of anybody."

A snort escapes Rudy. I glare at her as she desperately

tries to hold back a laugh. Her cheeks get bigger, and her eyes start to bulge; then the laugh escapes.

"A mean-old-ladies club?" she hollers, holding her stomach. "I can just imagine them in their nightgowns and head ties, sitting in a circle in their rocking chairs with a cauldron in the middle."

I have no idea what a cauldron is, but it sounds like something Juliette would have.

We are in the banana grove. I didn't realize we had gotten this far.

"They'll chant spells about all the children they hate." Rudy adopts this croaky voice, pinches her nose, and turns her lips downward. "Every night when all the children are asleep, we will pick out of a hat the name of which child to cast a spell on."

Rudy takes hold of my hands in the middle of the banana field. "Let's make up a song about them. I'm really good at making up songs." She screws up her face and wiggles her nose. Then she looks me deep in the eye and starts to chant.

Evil old ladies are here to say
We want Clara Dee to pay
Evil ladies every day chant
We want Rudy out the way.

I join in the chant. We skip in a circle, chanting louder, skipping faster and faster until we are so dizzy, we fall on the ground laughing.

I lay spread-eagled in the dirt, staring up at the night sky. I try to catch my breath.

"Will they be mad that we ran off?" Rudy asks.

I think about Mama's worried face as I read from the diary, knowing full well that her worry turned to anger when I ran off.

"I can't go back," I tell her. I feel her take my hand.

"We'll get in trouble together," she whispers. I remember her mother at Ms. Gee's, worried that I was walking home alone. She will blame me for taking Rudy with me.

I sigh, pulling my hand away. "You should go." I can't have another person mad at me. I just can't.

Rudy continues to stare at the sky, unfazed by me pulling away.

"You shouldn't let people make you so angry," she says. "My mother says if they make you angry, then they've won."

I turn my head to look at her. "Is that why she didn't get mad at Ms. Gee that night when I was over there?"

She nods, not looking away from the sky. "Mm-hmm."

I turn on my side to face her.

"Why didn't Ms. Gee tell anybody she had a daughter?"

Her chest rises and falls, and her hands link across her

chest. For moment, she says nothing. Then, as if making a firm decision, she turns on her side to face me. I make myself comfortable. This feels like it's going to be juicy.

"My nana and my grandpa fell out when Mom was fifteen. He got a job in New York, but Nana didn't want to leave Sycamore Hill. Mom said they asked her to choose. Stay in Sycamore with Nana or go to New York with Grandpa."

My heart beats fast, as if I didn't already know the ending. "She chose New York?"

Rudy nods. "It's not her fault," she mumbles. "They should never have made her choose."

"So Ms. Gee got mad?"

"She thought when Mom chose New York, she chose Grandpa and that meant Mom didn't love her anymore. So they stopped speaking. Your mom might remember her."

I think about Ms. Gee and how she pushes people away. Now it all makes sense.

"Mom kept trying to contact her, but she wouldn't answer her letters. She told me she didn't know how much longer Nana had left, so if she wouldn't answer our letters, we would go to her."

I've seen Ms. Gee's letters. I don't know who picks them up from the post office, but she makes us read them to her. I've never seen a letter from New York. Maybe Gaynah or Calvin did, but wouldn't they have mentioned it?

"I don't know if she received the letters."

I explain to Rudy how it works around here. Ms. Gee yells at us and we do things for her. If there was a letter from New York, we would know about it.

She shrugs. "Mom didn't like where we lived anyway. It wasn't good for me. She said it was time I saw where she came from and maybe we might like it and stay. But before we could even think about how to go about it, we got a letter out of the blue inviting us down. Mom isn't sure why Nana Gee sent the letter inviting us, though, because now we're here, she doesn't talk to Mom at all if she can help it."

Suddenly I feel very sorry for Rudy, this girl from New York. It's not easy dealing with Ms. Gee. Around here, we try not to take anything she says to heart, but I think I might take it to heart if she were my nana.

Rudy jumps to her feet suddenly. "Last one in the river turns into Juliette!" She darts through the trees. She peeks behind her to see me catching up and squeals, digging her feet in the dirt and pushing herself faster.

How weird she would change the subject like that. Maybe she doesn't want to talk about it. She's already fitting in. This town is full of things no one wants to talk about.

I catch her at the slope and we both run down it at full speed.

Rudy is squealing, "I can't stop." I veer into her, using her as a barrier. She does the same to me until we are entwined, holding on to each other and tumbling into the water. My trousers expand in the water. I look like an inflatable toy. Rudy points at me, laughing hysterically. I splash her, and her eyes widen in shock.

"Oh no you didn't!" She wades toward me, but the water pulls her back and she can't get to me fast enough. This makes us laugh harder.

"Can we join?" The voice comes from across the river. It's Calvin with his friend Anton.

Without waiting for an answer, Calvin rolls up his jeans and wades over, beaming from ear to ear. I withdraw a little, remembering he was with Gaynah laughing at me.

"Clara"—he is pointing down at my feet—"you're in water." I look down at my feet under the water. It isn't deep water, it only reaches my knees, but I back out as if a shark were coming toward me. I clamber to my feet and run up the hill, my eyes stinging with tears.

"Clara!" I hear Rudy call behind me, but I continue climbing until I reach the top. I am out of breath and my throat is stinging. I feel a hand on my shoulder. Rudy turns me to face her with her wet hands and water dripping from her clothes. She pulls me into a hug and now my face is wet, and I can smell the river on her.

I hear a rustle among the banana trees, and Uncle Albert appears, still in his gray work trousers and matching shirt. I don't think I've ever seen him wear anything else.

"Thought I would find you here," he says in his usual quiet voice. "Why you always running away, Clara?"

I lower my eyes to the ground. "Is Mama mad?"

He makes a noise in his throat that's neither a yes nor a no. He nods to Rudy. "I told your mother I'd keep an eye on you. Come, I'm going to see Leroy. Clara, you can show your friend your place."

I break into a wide smile, relieved he won't force me back to the party. I turn to Rudy. "I have something really cool to show you."

Her eyes widen, and they are a light brown with black specks. "Cooler than this night?" she cries.

I shake my head in dismay. This poor girl. I am about to blow her mind.

CHAPTER
NINE

MOST NIGHTS, WHEN HE HAS FINISHED work in the fields, Uncle Albert walks down the hill to his best friend's house, where they sit on the veranda overlooking the sea. They will talk about work and politics but mostly about how much fun they had when they were younger. How they ran the streets, how the music was better and people were kinder.

Sometimes, because Uncle Albert doesn't talk much, they just sit in silence listening to the sound of the waves hitting the wall that protects Leroy's house from the sea.

At eleven every night they say their goodbyes and he heads back up the hill and straight to bed, ready for work the next morning.

Tonight, he takes us through the banana grove on the path that the workers use. It gives easy access to the road without climbing the hill. The banana grove is so big that if you don't keep to the path, it's easy to get lost.

The moon shines on Uncle Albert's bald head, and the shadow of a banana leaf forms on his dark skin. We follow in a line, and I think how Uncle Albert has always been there for me in his own quiet way. How he always made sure he knew where I was without suffocating me. How good he is at keeping Mama happy while still leaving me be. How he made signs so I wouldn't forget what route to take when I would help him in the banana grove. He would pick all the bananas and tell me and Gaynah to pile them in the back of his truck. Then we would drive farther into the hills to get more.

The grove goes on for miles into the hills. It's owned by a businessman named Mr. Hyke, who I've only met once, when he came to check on his land.

Mr. Hyke lives in the city, and Uncle Albert says he has a big house with servants and a swimming pool.

There is only one road going into the hills, and it's barely drivable. It's full of potholes and big rocks, and it's so narrow that you can see the sheer drop over the edge. Only one other person lives that far into the hills: Papa's brother Eldorath. But Eldorath doesn't like people visiting him, not since Pastor Brown turned the town against him.

As we come out of the grove and onto Sycamore Hill by the junction, I almost forgive Uncle Albert for retrieving the memory box from the river.

I take the lead as we turn off East Avenue and down another steep but wider road. I know these roads like the back of my hand. I have walked these roads to school and with Uncle Albert when he knew I needed to get away.

East Avenue has four or five houses on either side with grassy front yards and big gardens. The houses here are closer together than ours, but it is obvious these people are the ones with the money. They have shiny American trucks parked in their driveways, and black BMWs.

We reach the end of East Avenue, and I point to our police station, tucked away on a dead end. "Anton's dad works there. He's the chief of police."

"It's so small," Rudy says in awe. "Our police station is ten times bigger, with hundreds of cops, and they drive around in their cars staring at you like this." She scrunches up her face to look as mean as possible. "They never leave us alone; they're always watching us." Her voice rises in waves of frustration and sadness.

We pass Phillip James Church, where Mama and Papa got married and I got baptized.

"Where I live," she continues, "there are some bad kids, but there are a lot more good kids, but the cops think we're all the same." I am torn between wanting to interrupt her to show her everything and wanting to know about her life in New York.

The road veers round a narrow bend and turns off down the hospital road. Rudy has stopped talking about home and is now transfixed once again by her surroundings. I point to the hospital as we pass the entrance, the crumbling stone surrounding it still not fixed after the last storm. "Mama used to work there, and my grandma."

"Why doesn't she work there anymore?" Her voice is gentle, as if somehow she knows the reason is sad. I am ashamed to tell her that I don't know. One day last year, she just stopped, and I never asked why.

"She just doesn't."

Rudy doesn't ask me anything more about it, and I change the subject, pointing ahead. There is an old guard post almost swallowed by overgrown grass. On either side of the path are two stone pillars that used to hold impressive gates, but the gates have gone, replaced by tufts of grass. Rudy spots the first cannon at the seawall and starts to screech words I can't make out.

Uncle Albert leaves us at his friend's gate and tells us to come and get him when we're ready to go home. I tell him

I will wave to him from the wall, and take Rudy's hand as we run through the gate.

Fort Charlotte is an old fighting fort that the English used to defend the island. It was built hundreds of years ago, when England ruled our island and they didn't want anyone else to have it.

The fort has fallen apart since then, but you can still recognize what it was. They're rusted and peeling and none of them works, but the four cannons facing the sea still stand tall. There are lookout points and oval windows cut out of stone. There is a wall surrounding the fort that you can walk on and see the entire town and ships far out to sea.

Gaynah was never interested in history or rusty cannons. I was afraid Rudy would turn her nose up at it, but she doesn't. She plays along.

Rudy goes to the first cannon, running her hand along it, her mouth wide open. She catches sight of the lookout posts and sticks her head through; then she runs up the steps to the wall and looks out across the bay. She turns and shouts down to me, "Ah ho! I see a ship! Get your men ready to fight."

My heart swells as I order my men to position their guns.

"Take aim. Fire!"

We pull back the cannons, sending cannonballs sailing across the water and straight into the unsuspecting ships.

"We have a hit! And another!"

"Look out for the boat below!" I warn.

She jumps down next to me. "Thank you, soldier." She pats me on the back. "Leave this one to me." She runs across the court, pretends to grab a gun, and sticks it through one of the windows. She fires, but her ammo is stuck. She calls for help. I leave my position, pick up my gun, and run to save her. I hand her a spare gun, and together we fire until everyone on the boat is dead.

The last ship explodes into the night sky like fireworks.

CHAPTER
TEN

AFTER AN EXHAUSTING GAME, WE SIT on the stone wall, our legs dangling over the edge. We are parched, and I wish I had grabbed a drink before we ran off. We could go to Uncle Albert's friend's house; he would have plenty of drinks. But that would mean leaving the fort, and I am not ready to leave yet.

Rudy crosses her legs, resting her elbows on her knees, staring out to the ocean.

"I'm so glad we came here." She sighs. "It's the best decision Mom ever made." I think about Ms. Gee and how angry she seems to be that Rudy and her mom have returned home, yet still, Rudy is happy to be here.

"I heard you don't remember anything about last year. Is that true?" she asks.

I pull my legs up to my chest and hold them close, as if the waves might rise up and take me. My chest closes in, and I don't know why she's asking me this. Gaynah must have been talking about me again. Telling people my business.

I feel Rudy take my hand, and she is smiling at me "It's okay. I don't remember things sometimes. My mom says it only happens when I don't want to do something, like make my bed or put the trash out. Selective memory, she calls it." She giggles and it forces me to smile.

We sit quietly with only the sound of the waves lapping onto the side of the wall.

"Did I tell you I want to be a Broadway star when I'm older?" She catches my blank face. "Broadway is a place with theaters and lights and hundreds of musicals on all the time. Some of the stages are big, some are small. Sometimes they have really big celebrities play there. If you want to be a star, that's where you have to go." She takes a breath. "What do you want to be when you grow up? A dancer, a singer, a movie star?" Her eyes grow wide. "A pirate?"

I am afraid to tell her I used to want to be a surfer. I don't think she would understand why a girl from Sycamore would want to surf. I told Mama once and she asked me why. I told her I didn't know why, I just knew that was what I wanted to do because I loved the water so much.

"I want to be a nurse, like Mama used to be," I tell her.

She beams. "That sounds like a perfect job."

I can't tell her what I really want to do. Rudy might be a nice person and she might understand. But if I tell her the truth, that I want to surf all over the world, she will want to know why I no longer surf, and I don't know why. I just know I'm afraid of the water now.

She stands. "Come on, Mrs. Nurse Woman. I heard there are hundreds of soldiers out there who need our help. Let's save them before our enemies get to them first."

And just like that she is running along the wall and down the steps to a new adventure.

The air feels thick like just before a storm when all the air is sucked out. The sky is a dark gray and the clouds are swollen, like they are about to burst. The water is slow at first. It creeps slowly into the room like a thief in the night. Then, out of nowhere, it grows tall and strong, hovering over my bed, threatening to take me under.

I wake up with a start, gasping for air. Stumbling out of bed, I fall to the floor, my head in my hands, waiting for the fog to clear. These flashbacks are getting more frequent and more frightening. I slip on my slippers and make my way out of the bedroom and into the living room, looking for Mama.

There is a weird air on the hill this morning. Kids are still playing, and dogs are still barking, but everything else feels different.

For a start, Papa is still home. Usually he would be bartering with the stall owners by now, trying to get the best price for the fish he caught that morning. Instead, he is out on the veranda with Mama, and they are talking in low voices. I can't hear what they're saying, but Papa is rubbing Mama's back, and she is shaking her head.

I decide to return to my room and stay out of the way. I've upset Mama enough already.

I spend the morning cleaning my board in my bedroom. Around lunchtime I hear Rudy's voice. I go outside and find her with her mother, talking to Mama and Papa.

"Clara." Rudy waves me over.

Mama and Papa seem startled to see me. Mama mumbles something about having so much to do today. "Clara, make sure you're not under my feet." And she slips by me into the house.

Papa gets to his feet, brushing his hands on his torn jeans, which have seen better days, but Papa doesn't like to buy new clothes. He says there are more important things to spend money on, like food.

He picks up a familiar basket from the veranda floor. "Be good," he says, and heads down the hill. I know where he's going, where he always goes this time of the week: to see his brother. Eldorath.

Rudy has noticed the weird air too. She said Ms. Gee actually let her mom cook her breakfast today, and on their way to my house this morning, Pastor Brown was praying on his porch. "His face was all screwed up like this"—she scrunches her face so her eyes are closed and her lips are pursed—"and he was begging for God's help."

I have a feeling that prayer was for me, but I don't tell Rudy that.

Today Rudy is wearing white pants that are splashed with red, green, yellow, and blue, as though she threw paint on it herself. Her hair is covered with a white bunny hat with two long ears that fall to her shoulders. She looks so cool, like nothing I've ever seen before.

"You look nice."

She beams. "Really? You think so?" She then goes into detail about why she chose that outfit today. Apparently, she doesn't just choose the first thing she sees, like I do. For Rudy, there is a story behind everything.

"Today I was feeling a little sad after the party. It started so nice, but then the happiness was taken away. So the paint on my clothes is me trying to bring back my happiness. You know? Like I'm saying no to sadness." She wags her finger at the air with an exaggerated frown.

I don't know what to say to that.

"O . . . kay" is all I muster.

"I like what you're wearing," she continues, taking in my old blue shorts and black T-shirt. "It really suits you."

I frown, looking down at myself. "It does?"

She nods. "Yep. Blue is definitely your color." No one's ever said they liked what I was wearing. I imagine Gaynah's face if she were here. She would scoff at Rudy and tell her she was clearly still jet-lagged from the plane.

I climb off the veranda wall we have been sitting on. "Want to know a secret?"

Her eyes light up. "Yes!"

So I take her somewhere I've never taken anyone before except Gaynah. I take her to my secret dugout.

I'm nervous she might not like it. Rudy is so loud, and everything is so big to her that maybe my hideout will be a letdown. I have nothing to worry about, though, because when I show her, she jumps up and down, screeching.

"Is it your secret hideout? Like a cave where you keep hidden treasures?"

"Um . . . not really."

"Oh, are we pirates with stolen gold and we have to hide it before the gun-shooting soldiers come after us?"

I can't help but feed into her imagination. "No, it's from the plantation owner in the big house behind the banana grove. There's treasure on that land and it's ours. He stole it from us. We need to get it back."

Her eyes widen. "Eighteen hundreds role play. I love it." She clasps her hands together and paces outside the dugout. "How will we get the rest of the gold and our freedom? We must get the gold. Then we must burn his house down. We can't have him coming after us. Which way to the evil owner?"

I stare at her blankly. I don't know anyone evil. But I do know someone with a big plantation house that fits in with her game. Eldorath.

Three generations of our family have lived in that house on the hill. When the British left, the owners abandoned it, and Eldorath and Papa's great-grandfather, who used to work on the land, took it over. Now Eldorath lives there by himself.

Rudy is insistent we play the game, so I play along, for now.

We gather supplies from the kitchen: a bottle of water, some leftover ackee and salt fish from breakfast, and some coconut cookies.

I don't tell Rudy no one goes to Eldorath's house except Papa. I don't tell her that my heart is beating superfast and my legs feel wobbly at the thought of going there.

CHAPTER
ELEVEN

PAPA NEVER TALKS ABOUT THE DAY he left the house on the hill. All I know is he left and only went back to visit Eldorath. Now, sometimes he says he's going to trim the trees because the last time he went, the branches were too long. Other times he says he's going to tidy the garden because if he doesn't do it, no one will. Then there are the times he doesn't say why he's going. He just goes, and when I ask if I can go with him, the answer is always the same: "Not today."

I try to put Rudy off going to Eldorath's house because I don't want to get in trouble with Papa.

"Are you sure you want to do this?"

She lays a gentle hand on my shoulder as we stand in

the middle of the banana grove. "Dearest sister," she says, still pretending to be a rebellious girl from the 1800s, "it is our duty. For Papa, Mama, and for our country."

I sigh, turning away from the river and looking through the trees toward the hill. I've noticed that when Rudy plays a game, she takes it seriously. Luckily, Uncle Albert is nowhere to be seen.

"I wish I had worn my petticoat dress and my bonnet," she says. "Then I could have looked the part."

"You really have one of those?"

"Mm-hmm. It's baby blue with white trim. My mom bought it for me at the vintage market."

"Your mom is nice."

"She is. She works a lot, so I don't see her very much back home." She sighs like an adult who has the world on their shoulders. "Maybe we can stay here and then I might see her more."

She falls silent and I have to turn to make sure she is still with me. "You okay?"

She forces a smile. "Mm-hmm."

We reach the end of the banana grove and stop. The hill continues upward into thick forest, but we take a break and have a drink of water. Rudy stares at the view in awe. We can see the entire banana grove from here, and in the middle of it all I see Calvin and Gaynah heading our way.

Great. Mama probably told them that we were down here. What do they want, anyway? I really wasn't in the mood for Calvin and his wannabe sidekick, Gaynah.

I shove the bottle of water in my backpack and nudge Rudy. "Let's go. My so-called friends are coming."

"Should we wait?"

"No," I snap. "Don't you remember what they did? They laughed at what you were wearing at the river."

Rudy looks taken back. "They did?"

I bite my lip. "Also, what about last night?"

"But that was the adults," she says. "And whatever they did to you, Clara, maybe they've come to say sorry."

She's wrong. "They haven't come to say sorry."

"How do you know that?"

Because I know them.

Calvin reaches us out of breath, Gaynah a ways behind him. "Where are you two going?" he says between breaths. He points down the hill. "I thought you were at the river, but . . ."

"What do you want, Calvin?"

Gaynah has reached us now, and she won't even look me in the eye. Calvin searches for some story they have concocted together.

"Sorry," he says, "about last night. My dad, he gets a bit much sometimes. You know that."

I glare at Gaynah, but she stares at the ground.

"Right," I say, turning toward the hill. "Thanks for coming. See you around." I begin the climb into the forest, Rudy hesitantly looking behind her as she walks alongside me.

"Where are you going?" Calvin calls after us.

"We're looking for loyalty," I snap, "and real friends. I heard they're out here somewhere." I take Rudy's hand and pull her away.

Rudy is quiet for the next ten minutes, which is unlike her, so I guess she is mad at me. I feel a little guilty for upsetting her, but having Calvin and Gaynah follow us to Eldorath's is not my idea of fun. Mama and Papa have been clear: I'm not supposed to go there, so I definitely don't want those two tagging along.

We plow through the trees. There are no paths to follow, but I reckon if we keep going forward, we are bound to find it. It's hard to miss. After a while I can see that Rudy is struggling to keep up. I suggest we take a break by a small creek that weaves down the hill. She is grateful and smiles for the first time since we left Calvin and Gaynah.

We sit in the dirt and share Mama's leftovers and the last bit of water.

"You're so lucky, going where you want whenever you want," Rudy says. "In New York, I can't go anywhere by myself. My mom wouldn't allow it."

Going places by myself isn't something I've ever thought about. Sycamore Hill is home, all of it. From our backyard to Ms. Gee's house, to the fort to the river. It's all home. The only place I know I'm not allowed to go is Eldorath's house.

"It's home." I shrug, drinking some water. "It's not like going into the city; everyone knows me here."

She stares into the distance, filling her mouth with cookies. "I think your hideout might be the best thing I have ever seen. The next-best thing is the fort, and maybe this will be our third-best thing."

I smile weakly. "Mm-hmm."

After we eat, Rudy comes to life. She wants to know how we are going to extract the gold, and should we set fire to the land before or after?

I am grateful to see her back to herself again and play along.

"Well, after, or we might get caught in the fire."

She nods in agreement. The bushes are becoming thick and almost unpassable, so I use a stick to push through the thick undergrowth and my shoes to flatten the ground.

"How big is his land? It might take us days to find the gold."

I am hoping she doesn't really expect me to dig Eldorath's land. Mama will kill me if she knows I've been up here, never mind that we also dug up his land, but I'm not sure how far Rudy is planning to take this. I'm thinking I might have to put a stop to this soon.

After a few minutes of forcing our way through thick bushes, we see it through a line of trees: a large old house with peeling walls that still looks beautiful in an antique kind of way. I've been here before, not through the trees where Rudy and I came, but on the potholed road that leads from Sycamore town past our houses and weaves up the hill to Eldorath's. The road gets less passable the farther you go. By the time you reach Eldorath's house, it's practically impossible to drive. I've followed Papa up that road a few times without him knowing. He's one of the only people who come this way, but he does it at least once a week with a basket filled with fish he has caught and fruits from our garden. Sometimes he carries a bulla cake or some coconut drops, but he always comes alone to see his brother Eldorath.

The house is grand, but it stands against a dark shadow from the tall trees surrounding it. The garden is messy and overgrown. Papa must not have cut it for some time. Or maybe he can't keep up.

Rudy grabs my hand. "Come on."

I pull back, mortified. "What? No? We can't actually go digging in his garden."

I would be in so much trouble.

She rolls her eyes. "Of course not, silly. We're going to explore first. Then we dig."

She pulls me through the trees and out into the open, where anyone can see us. I start to panic. "I'm not sure about this, Rudy," I say, but she marches forward, dragging me with her. I imagine what Papa will say when he finds out we have been here. I don't like upsetting him, but there is something magnetic about Rudy and her adventures.

CHAPTER
TWELVE

THE HOUSE GETS BIGGER AS WE move through the long grass. There are two floors. The front of the house sticks out from the sides like a disjointed Rubik's Cube. I count the windows to calm my nerves. Eight at the top, and eight at the bottom. The closer we get, the taller the house seems. I wonder if Eldorath is watching us from one of those windows. Or is he already out here, waiting for his moment to demand why we are on his land?

I grip Rudy's hand tighter. "I really don't think this is a good idea."

"Don't worry," Rudy whispers, sensing my fear, "I went to six classes of karate, but then they told me I couldn't come back if I didn't wear the right uniform. It was no fun without my tutu, so I gave it up. But I know how to defend myself, so you have nothing to worry about."

I picture Rudy in a pink tutu, learning karate, and it is enough to make me giggle. My laughing soon stops when I hear a rustle behind us. We stop abruptly and listen. Yes, someone is coming toward us. Rudy points two fingers to her eyes, and I focus on her as hard as I can. She holds up three fingers and mouths the words *Three, two, one*. Before I can ask what she's doing, she jumps in front of me with a scream, kicking her left leg out in the air. Nothing. She spins around, her bunny hat spinning with her. She listens, then runs into the grass screaming, "Come out, you scaredy-cat!"

Seconds later she returns with a sheepish Calvin and Gaynah. I give an almighty groan, throwing my hands in the air. "You have to be kidding me."

"You guys are having all the fun," Calvin says. He pleads, "Come on, Clara. Nothing happens on Sycamore. I don't see you at the beach anymore. Now you two are having all these adventures, and I want to join in."

Gaynah folds her arms across her chest, turning away. "He wanted to come here," she huffs. "Not everyone wants a membership in the Clara fan club."

My lips screw together. I am about to remind her of her Calvin membership, but Rudy steps between us. She looks me dead in the eye. "Remember what I said down at the river?"

I count under my breath. "Fine."

"So, is that a yes?" Calvin asks, his voice rising with excitement.

I shrug. "Whatever."

Rudy asks if she can explain the plan. I tell her she can do what she wants. It's not as if they're leaving anytime soon. She plants herself in the middle of us and tells Calvin and Gaynah our plan to steal the gold. They stare at her blankly. Gaynah cries out in disbelief, "We've come all this way to play make-believe?"

But Calvin beams at me, then at Rudy. "I'm in."

"I heard he never leaves his house except for Saturday afternoon, when he goes to the fish market to buy fish for his hungry ghosts," Calvin hisses as we tiptoe toward the house. I shoot him a look and he shrinks back, sheepish. "Sorry."

As we get closer to the house, I keep thinking about Calvin's story, and it hits hard. I never did like hearing the rumors about my uncle, especially as none of them made sense. The stories had got out of hand over the years. At first, he was just a man who saw ghosts. Now he was a witch doctor who used his magic to feed children to his ghosts. The stories got worse and worse, and I knew who was behind it: Pastor Brown.

I almost moan to Gaynah about Calvin annoying me, but I remember just in time that Gaynah is not my friend. She lingers a few feet behind us, still pretending she doesn't want to be here. We gather near the steps to the house, where there is an oval entrance with a dark door. I spot Papa's food basket left on the doorstep. He must have been already. Or maybe he is cutting Eldorath's garden around the back. I scan the grounds for him.

"I think maybe we should see if the proprietor is home," Rudy whispers. "One cannot risk being found out before we find the treasure."

Calvin nods along with a serious frown on his face. "Yes, agreed."

Still crouching, Rudy presses her back against the wall and moves slowly to the back of the house. I am behind her, Calvin behind me and Gaynah at the rear. The house is silent. Nothing but the crunch of stones under our feet. I half expect to see Papa appear around the corner, shaking his head in dismay as he does when I've done something that doesn't please him. There is nothing but silence.

At the back of the house is a large sycamore tree and a garden that goes on for miles. You can see spots where Papa has tried to cut the grass, but it is clearly too much for just him, because even the parts he cut are now catching up with the rest that merge into the forest. Calvin points to steps leading up to the house. Spiraling staircases that meet on a balcony. Another set of stairs go downward underneath the house. Before anyone can stop him, Calvin runs down the steps and disappears.

"It's open," he hisses.

Rudy is not far behind him. She stops halfway down, beckoning us to follow. I turn to Gaynah, and she is under the sycamore tree.

"I'm not going in there," she says flatly. "You want to get your tongue cut out by the voodoo man, you go, but I like my tongue, thank you."

"That's my uncle you're talking about," I snap. But I don't tell her I am just as nervous to enter.

I bite my tongue and debate my options. Stay out here in the open with Gaynah or go inside Eldorath's house. Reluctantly I join Rudy on the stairs. I would rather be in the house with Rudy than out here with Gaynah. Rudy and I link hands and enter the house together.

Calvin is waiting for us in what looks like a cellar. The ceiling is low, with just enough room for us to walk upright. I tighten my grip on Rudy's hand as we look around, barely breathing. There is an old dresser with a large mirror over it and black-and-white pictures of the house on the walls. I nudge Rudy, pointing to wooden stairs leading upstairs.

I can hear my heart beating against my chest. Rudy

drags me over to the stairs. She nods upward. Calvin squeezes next to me, and we crane our necks to look. There is a door at the top of the stairs that leads to the rest of the house.

"The proprietor is most likely up there," Rudy whispers, still in character.

I shake my head at her, waving my hand under my neck to cut the performance. Calvin agrees with me. The game is over. We can no longer pretend we are here to steal gold. This is real. We are inside Eldorath's house uninvited, and if we get caught, we are going to be in big trouble.

CHAPTER
THIRTEEN

"I'M NOT GOING UP THERE," CALVIN whispers when we try to decide who will go up the stairs first. We both look to Rudy. She shrugs. "I don't mind talking to the owner. I bet he has lots to tell us about his house."

Calvin turns to me. "It's between you and me, then. Rock paper scissors?"

I shake my head. "No. I'll go." I figure we are already inside the house. If we leave now, we might never get this chance again. Plus, Eldorath is family. Maybe if he sees me first, he'll take pity on us and not tell our parents.

Besides, what else would we do today? Go to the river? Play pick leaf? It's only two weeks into the summer, and I've already had enough of both.

I feel someone grab my top as I climb the stairs and

assume it's Rudy losing her nerve, but when I reach the top, Calvin is right behind me, still grabbing onto me.

"What are you doing?" I whisper.

He lets go of me. "I'm scared."

"You're the one who went in here."

"I know, but now we're going *in* in."

I wrap my fingers around the doorknob and turn it slowly. Deep down I'm not sure what I am more afraid of: Eldorath finding us in his house uninvited or Papa finding out I was here.

I push the door gently; it creaks, sending chills down my back. I peer through the gap to try to see what is on the other side. There are wooden stairs going up to another floor. Underneath the stair, I see a chair against a fabric-covered wall. I push the door a little farther, listening for any noise. Footsteps, music, talking, Papa. Nothing but Calvin breathing heavily down my neck. I swat him away.

The hallway is dark, like the inside of Ms. Gee's house. Except this is a hundred times bigger. To the right is the front door; across from the stairs, a room. Farther down the hall, more rooms.

I find myself tiptoeing toward the room by the stairs. I can see the legs of a piano covered by a white cloth. The room is empty apart from the piano and a few chairs dotted around. There are pictures on the wall, also covered.

Rudy gasps at the size of the room. She runs around,

touching everything, peering under cloths, and finally pulling the cloth that covers the piano. Dust flies into the air, sending her into a coughing fit, her rabbit hat almost slipping off her head. The room echoes with her cough and, and the sound seems to linger in the air long after. Calvin shoots me a frightened look, and I know what he is thinking: Eldorath must have heard us.

We freeze like statues waiting for heavy footsteps and Eldorath's angry voice demanding who is in his house.

But no one comes.

Rudy brushes the seat clean with the back of her hand and sits down in front of the piano. She places her fingers on the keys and starts to play a song I have never heard. Her fingers fly across the piano in a perfect upbeat, and she sings the words at the top of her voice.

That's when I remember. Rudy's dream. She wanted to sing, but I didn't know she could sing. I didn't know she could play either, but she is beautiful at both.

I watch, mesmerized, as her hands move up and down in perfect coordination, her voice a perfect pitch that fills the room. If Papa were here, he would sit next to her with his guitar and sing along. I look around, wondering if he has been in this room and filled this empty house with music in the same way.

Calvin approaches me. "Dance?"

Rudy throws us a look of happiness over her shoulder and I suddenly think of Gaynah. I wonder where she is and if she is still waiting against the sycamore tree or if she got bored and left. I wish she had come in with us.

I allow Calvin to take my hand. He spins me around the empty floor. Round and round, until I say, "Stop, I'm dizzy." I spin back toward him, and he dips me to the floor before bringing me back up. I let go of his hand and twirl round and round the room on my own. Something about Rudy's playing and this old house makes me want to spin forever. I spread my arms out wide and spin across every inch of the floor.

The music stops suddenly, but I carry on. With my eyes closed, I spin, laughing at how freeing it feels. It's as if I have been stuck in a box and now the lid has been lifted off. I bump into Calvin and he grabs me before I fall.

"Clara!"

I open my eyes and we are not alone. Gaynah is in the room, looking frightened. Behind her is a man frowning.

It's Eldorath.

He is wearing a purple velvet suit with the longest jacket I have ever seen and a matching velvet hat that sits on the side of his head. Despite my fear of being caught, I wonder how he manages to wear it all without collapsing under the heat.

His dark skin is shiny and smooth, like he uses Vaseline on it the same way Mama uses it to oil my scalp. His face is long and narrow just the way I remember, with dark eyes that pierce into you. He has traces of a mustache and beard that connect at the sides of his mouth. The hairs in his beard are a mix of silver and black like he is getting old, but not Ms. Gee old.

The room is painfully quiet until Rudy jumps to her feet and slams the lid of the piano. I grimace at the thundering sound it makes in the silence.

Eldorath moves around a petrified Gaynah into the middle of the room. He turns slowly, looking each of us dead in the eye. I fix my eyes on the floor when he comes to me.

Please don't tell Papa, please don't tell Papa.

"Well? Anyone going to speak? Or are we all going to ignore the fact that children I did not invite are standing inside my house?"

He rolls each word under his tongue like Ms. Anderson, our math teacher, does.

"We were exploring," Rudy blurts out.

"In my house?"

She nods enthusiastically. "Because your house is so big and beautiful. Where else would we have an adventure?"

His eyes travel over her slowly from top to bottom, as

if he's trying to figure out what a girl with a New York accent is doing in his house.

I hold my breath, afraid to breathe in case it is too loud and he picks on me next.

Calvin edges toward the door. I think that's the best idea he's had yet and follow him.

"And who are you?" he says finally.

Rudy puffs her chest out. "Rudy."

"Rudy what?"

"Rudy McPhee, and these are my friends."

Eldorath's eyes linger on Gaynah, then on Calvin, forcing Calvin to scratch his head, pretending he wasn't trying to leave. Eldorath looks at Gaynah for so long, I think that maybe she might be the first to get in trouble. Then his eyes fall on me. I feel my body stiffen and I try to speak but no words come out.

Finally, he turns back to Rudy, and Calvin lets out a visible sigh of relief. He tries to hide his shaking hands behind his back.

"And what adventures did you find on my private land?"

"Treasures. You stole our gold, so we came to get it back."

I shake my head frantically at Rudy. Out of the corner of my eye, I see Gaynah and Calvin doing the same. But Rudy pays us no attention and continues to tell him everything. How we were going to dig up his garden for the rest of the gold he stole, then we would set it on fire so he could never steal from us again.

I groan inwardly. Well, if we weren't going to get in trouble before, we're definitely going to be in trouble now.

As if to confirm my fears, he marches out the door. "Follow me, all of you." He marches up the stairs with Rudy, wide-eyed and excited, on his tail. Calvin, Gaynah, and I are a little more hesitant. If there is a way to get out of trouble, we are going to find it.

Gaynah stops at the bottom of the stairs and nudges me. She nods toward the front door. We could escape now. We're close enough to make a run for it. Eldorath doesn't speak to anyone on the hill, so it would be like we were never here.

The sudden lack of footsteps from Eldorath and Rudy forces us to look upward. Eldorath looks down over the balcony. "Come along."

I force one foot in front of the other up the stairs until we reach the landing. Eldorath floats across the floor like a ghost. The second-floor landing has more chairs against the wall, and paintings of black men and women dressed in old-fashioned clothes and weird hats. Eldorath throws open a pair of double doors.

"Rudy, no!" I shout. But it is too late; she is throwing

herself into a room full of costumes. I could escape now, as they both enter the room that looks like a walk-in closet. Gaynah and Calvin would follow me without question, and Eldorath doesn't speak to Papa anyway. If we leave now, we might get away with it. If we stay, we are more likely to bump into Papa.

I hesitate at the doorway. Eldorath is distracted by Rudy's squeals. I look down the stairs to the front door, then back at Rudy.

The others look to me for the okay, while Rudy disappears into a row of clothes. I can't leave her here by herself.

"So." Eldorath spins around to face us. Our chance is gone. "What era is this adventure, eighteen hundred? Nineteen hundred? The seventies? I have it all."

Rudy looks over at me, her eyes so wide, I think they're about to pop out of her head. I take a deep breath. "Eighteen hundred," I say, stepping inside the room. "We've come to take our land back."

CHAPTER
FOURTEEN

EVERY TIME ELDORATH DISAPPEARS INTO A rack of clothes, Gaynah hisses, "He's going to kill us." I've never believed the rumors that my uncle was dangerous, and I believe it even less now that he stands in front of me. The witch doctor everyone is afraid of is not the same man who's running around trying to find the perfect dress for Rudy. There are no signs of sacrifices, no ghosts floating in the house, no threats to feed us to the dead.

It's strange how differently people view Eldorath and Papa. The hill looks up to Papa as one of their leaders. Whenever we have a storm, which is frequent on the island, he organizes the preparations, gets the wood to cover windows, bottles of water in case the road gets blocked, food to keep us going for a few weeks.

When his boat was damaged in the last storm, the village gathered to help him repair it, just as he helped them rebuild their houses. That's who he is. Who we are. Yet somehow, Eldorath didn't get that same treatment, and no one could tell me why except to repeat rumors of things they had never seen, only heard.

"Mama says all kinds of bad things happen here," Gaynah whispers in my ear. "She says you need a Bible and a cross before you enter." As if I weren't getting the point, she hisses, "He sacrifices children."

When I don't answer, she huffs, moving away from me and closer to Calvin. "Well, you might want to die here, but I don't."

I wave her away the same way she has done to me so many times.

She glances out the door, then back at Eldorath as she contemplates which is worse: to go back through the forest alone or to stay here with us. "Calvin will come with me."

I turn to Calvin. "Are you leaving?"

Calvin looks over at me. "Are you?"

I shake my head. "Not without Rudy."

His nose scrunches as he thinks. "All of us or none of us, then, I suppose."

Gaynah storms over to a seat under the window and plonks herself on it, pouting.

* * *

Eldorath has found costumes for all of us, even Calvin. He says he loved clothes so much, he ordered as many as he could from abroad. It became his full-time hobby, and sewing costumes for the theater in the city is his full-time job. This is enough to send Rudy over the edge. She skips through Eldorath's garden in a purple ball gown and her rabbit hat and shoots theater questions to him.

Eldorath puts me in a black high-collared dress and Calvin in a blue tailcoat and top hat. Gaynah refuses to dress up. We all look silly—the clothes don't fit us; they are too big and too fussy—but as we stroll through the long grass of Eldorath's garden, we can't help but fall under the spell.

Eldorath tells us about the party of the year he will be holding and how we must attend wearing our very best. I think he must be pretending for Rudy's sake, because this house hasn't held a party since I was born.

Rudy forgets about the gold we are supposed to be digging and links arms with him, agreeing that she would not miss it for the world.

Somehow, they suit each other, Rudy and Eldorath. They have the same imagination, and it's as if they have been waiting for each other their whole lives.

I catch up with them and ask why he never comes to the village anymore, or Mama's parties or church.

He squints at me. "Why, what is it you have heard?"

I look behind me at Gaynah shaking her head. I turn back, forcing a smile. "That you like to be by yourself."

A smile pulls at the corner of his mouth and he links his arm with mine. "I'm sure you heard more than that, but yes, I do like solitude. One cannot go wrong with his own company. But it was not entirely voluntary, for reasons we shall not talk about." He winks, placing a finger to his lips.

We stop under the sycamore tree to get some shade. I want to ask him what he means, and if the rumors are true, but Rudy pulls him away to ask him if there was gold here, where would it be buried?

Later, Eldorath makes us cheese sandwiches on hard dough bread and fruit punch in large wineglasses. We sit in his dining room around a long dark wood table that still feels empty even with us all around it.

"Why do people call you the witch doctor?" Rudy blurts out, her mouth full of food. The room tenses and my heart sinks. Sometimes I wish Rudy wouldn't say everything she thinks.

Eldorath clasps his hands in front of him. "That's a very good question," he says slowly. "This town never did like anything different, so they concoct stories to make people afraid."

Calvin and I exchange looks. By "people" he means Pastor Brown. He doesn't believe in ghosts; he thinks they're the work of the devil. It's hard to listen to Pastor Brown on a Sunday morning talking about the witch doctor in our midst. About how seeing ghosts is the work of the devil, and we will suffer the consequences of God if we go near him. It's hard to hear him talk about my uncle that way. It's even harder to watch my parents allow it.

Calvin lowers his sandwich to his plate, suddenly losing his appetite. I know what he is feeling because I am feeling it too. For so long we have been told stories about Eldorath. I've never found out if they're true or not because I was never allowed. Papa simply tells me to not listen to idle gossip, but he's never answered any of my questions.

"No one likes me because I'm different," Rudy says. She lays her hand on his. "But I don't care. My mom says if we are all the same, how will we stand out?"

The room explodes with Eldorath's clapping. "Bravo, Rudy McPhee." Rudy's smile is as wide as the table, and she doesn't stop smiling for the rest of the meal.

When we have finished eating, Eldorath tells us it is time to go home because our parents will be worried. He walks us to the forest.

"Well, I know what's different about Rudy," Eldorath says. "She is vibrant, bubbly, and unique, and she loves to dress up. What about the rest of you?"

Calvin half turns as he walks ahead. "I play cricket. I

might even get on the national team if I work hard enough. And I surf sometimes." He glances over at me, but I look away.

As Rudy and Calvin walk ahead, Eldorath turns to me. "And you, Clara?"

I shrug, a little embarrassed. Rudy is unique; Calvin plays for the Under 16s; even Gaynah sounds special with her gifts from America. There is nothing special about me.

"I sometimes say things I shouldn't say," I tell him. Out of the corner of my eye, Gaynah nods in agreement. "People don't like me much for that. Also, I forget things. Not everything, just certain things." Like things that happened last year.

We reach the edge of the forest, and Eldorath waves us off, inviting us back whenever we want, as long as our parents give us permission. I trail behind the others, then stop and run back. "Eldorath, I'm—"

He stops me with a hand on my shoulder. "Clara." He smiles warmly. "Your father was right. You are very special. I'm going to help you realize that. Let's not leave it so long next time."

I walk into the woods, feeling a weird chill down my spine, wondering what my father may have told him.

When we reach the banana grove, we make a pact to not tell anyone about our secret visit to Eldorath. We agree that no one would understand, that they don't know Eldorath like we do.

Calvin and Gaynah say goodbye and continue straight toward the road. I climb the hill to my house with Rudy.

We reach the yard and walk around the house to the veranda. Rudy's mom, Mama, and Papa jump to their feet when they see us. "Where have you been?" Mama cries. "And what are you wearing?"

I look down at the black dress Eldorath let me keep. Oh no. I forgot we were wearing his clothes. I try to think of something believable, but the dress clearly gives me away.

"We saw Eldorath," Rudy blurts out.

I elbow her in the ribs and whisper, "Really? You can't tell one lie?"

She slips her hand into mine, pulling me beside her. I glance up at Mama and Papa, who are staring at me with eyebrows raised. I sigh in surrender.

"Fine. We went to see him, and I know I'm not allowed to, but he's a really nice man. He has a huge room filled with clothes from the eighteen hundreds and a coat from the seventies. So we think you all owe him an apology."

Rudy squeezes my arm. "I couldn't have said it better myself."

Mama's and Papa's mouths fall open. Neither of them can find the words to speak.

* * *

I am climbing into bed when Mama pulls the curtains to one side and enters my room. She waits until I sit up in the bed before sliding in behind me, her legs on either side of mine. She pulls the comb through my hair, parting it in the middle to make braids for the night.

"You think your papa and I are wrong to not let you see Eldorath." It is more a statement than a question, and I'm not sure if she wants me to answer, so I stay silent waiting for the but, the telling-off, the explanation for why I am not allowed up there.

"Did anything happen?" Her voice is the smallest I've ever heard it. Does she believe in the witch-doctor story too?

"No, Mama," I tell her, hoping that this means I can now see Eldorath. "The only person who didn't like being there was Gaynah, but I think that's because of what her mom says to her. She always says mean things."

She stops braiding my hair. "What things?" she asks. "What things did Gaynah say?"

I shrug, fidgeting with the sheet between my fingers. I don't want to get Gaynah in any more trouble, even if we aren't friends. I think I've said enough things about her, and I don't want to become the bad person myself.

"Clara?"

But I also want people to stop being mean to Eldorath, because he's done nothing wrong, and I want to be able to go to his house again.

"She said her mom told her he worships the devil."

"And?" Her voice trembles.

"And he sacrifices children."

"She said this today? At the house?"

I nod, biting my lip. I can tell by Mama's tone things are about to kick off. I don't understand why she's so mad now. This isn't news. Juliette has been saying this for years, so why is she mad now?

As if she has had enough of the conversation, she quickly finishes off my hair and stands, smoothing her skirt.

"So can I see Eldorath again?" I wait with held breath, begging her to say yes.

"No."

"Even if he wants to see me?"

She stops by the door and turns, lines edged into her usually smooth skin. "Clara," she says tiredly, "do as I say and don't go there anymore."

She disappears behind the curtains that separate my room from the living room. I sink into the bed, hands clenched into fists, my mind racing. Eldorath said we could visit again, I know he did, so what is Mama hiding from me?

CHAPTER
FIFTEEN

MAMA WAKES ME EARLY AND I think something must have happened because I just went to bed. She tells me we are going to the city. As my eyes adjust to the darkness, I see she is already dressed. "Hurry," she says. "We have a long drive." I am confused but too sleepy to argue.

I throw on my only pair of jeans and a jacket with some old black sneakers that I have had for years and are pulling open at the sides. I grab the white bunny hat Rudy let me borrow and slip it on my head, even though I know it will make my ears sweat.

When I step out onto the veranda, Papa is sitting on the wall with his back to me. Mama has her arm around his shoulders.

"Are you sure?" Mama is asking him. Papa doesn't say anything for a while. Finally, he rubs his lips. "I don't know the answer to that, Alysa, but I think it is time." He turns to her quizzically. "Don't you?" His face changes when he spots me. He forces a smile.

"Ready?" Papa asks brightly.

"What's going on?" I ask, confused.

Papa hooks his arm round my neck and leads me down the hill. "We're going on an adventure. You like adventures, don't you?"

I think he must be talking about yesterday. This feels like a trick. "I think so."

He chuckles, patting my head. "Of course you do. Come on, time is ticking."

Papa says Pastor Brown lent him his car, which is surprising considering they were arguing on Mama's birthday.

I don't know what is going on. One minute Mama is upset with me for going to Eldorath's house; the next minute they are taking me to the city. I turn to Mama as she joins us. "Why?"

I catch them exchanging a look. "It's the summer," Mama says cheerily. "We thought a trip to the city might be fun."

She ushers me into the backseat of the car. She and Papa get in the front, and we move off down the hill.

The car reaches town, and we take the traffic circle

along the sea road. I wind my window down and stick my hand out. Papa turns on the radio and starts singing along to the song that's playing, even though he doesn't know all the words. I inhale the fresh air and close my eyes.

You know right away when you're in the city. The air changes from fresh and clean to thick and heavy. Our car slows down, and someone presses on their horn, waking me. We are stuck in traffic. Papa huffs and puffs just like all the other drivers. Mama tells him to calm down. It's only been a few minutes since we got here, and he is already losing it.

Papa hates the city. I don't know why he brought me here. He says when he thinks of hell, he imagines it's something like city life. Too many people, polluted air, and congestion.

"People are not kind in the city," he says.

After twenty long minutes in traffic, Papa parks the car outside a white one-story building. It sits next to a line of stores and across from the beach. As soon as Papa parks the car, we throw open the doors for some much-needed air, except the air outside is just as stifling. I look around me, confused. "Where are we?"

They don't answer.

We walk through the parking lot and through automatic doors. The air-conditioning hits us like a full-blown hair dryer belting out ice-cold air. I collapse on the ground with relief. Mama tells me to get up off the dirty floor.

"But it's so cool."

She grabs my arm, pulling me to my feet. "Did you not see the shoes that were walking on it? Those shoes just came from outside, and outside is not clean. Now come along."

We pass people in white chairs, all with sad faces, quietly staring off into the distance, their eyes vacant, except for a woman chatting nonstop to anyone who will listen and an old man telling the woman behind a desk that he is Jesus. It's as if they were waiting to be seen by the doctor, but this is no hospital. There were no signs outside or inside on the walls.

We hurry along white sanitized halls and up some wide tiled stairs where a picture of Jesus is hung on the wall. In it, Jesus is sitting behind a long table with his disciples on either side of him. Where the stairs split, we turn to the right and follow a long corridor. I count the doors as we pass them. Each door has a name on it like Bishop Anderson, Bishop Frankly, Bishop Amos. I forget to count and try to peer through one of the keyholes.

"Mama, are we at church?"

We stop outside a door that says BISHOP MASON. Mama knocks on the door.

"Come in."

We enter a large room with wide windows and a fan attached to the ceiling. It makes a whirring noise that sounds like insects flying around your ears.

I only see Bishop Mason once a year. When we have the friendly parish competitions. Except it's not friendly; they only call it friendly because it's between churches. Each village competes to win best in the parish.

We play games that only the adults enjoy, like cricket or dominoes. There are stalls with food cooked by our best cooks. There is a talent show too, but we never win. The only thing I remember about Bishop Mason is how he moves his mustache side to side with his mouth. He does this when he is thinking and after he has laughed at his own joke. His mustache is very distracting and often makes me forget to listen to him when he is talking.

He shakes Mama's and Papa's hands but doesn't take his eyes off me, even when Mama or Papa is talking. They tell him that Pastor Brown recommended they come to him. Why are Mama and Papa listening to Pastor Brown?

Bishop Mason nods repeatedly. "Yes, yes."

He narrows his eyes at me. "And who is this?"

"Clara," I say.

"*Clara?*" he repeats.

Bishop Mason asks a lot of obvious questions. Like, "What's the weather like out there, hot?" when he's got a perfectly good window with the sun shining in. Or, "Are you on summer break?" No, I'm in school right now. Hi, teacher.

Bishop Mason is not much taller than me, and he is smaller than Rudy, because she is at least an inch taller than me. He tells Mama and Papa to wait outside on the row of plastic seats. As soon as the door closes, he points to the bunny hat on my head and says, "First, take that off."

CHAPTER
SIXTEEN

I DON'T KNOW BISHOP MASON VERY well, except from
what I already mentioned. I do know that he is the big
boss of our church. He is higher up than Pastor Brown and
looks after all the churches in our parish. That's all I know.
I don't know what he does when he's not preaching. I don't
know if he's kind or mean. I don't know if he meant to tell
me to take off the bunny hat like Ms. Gee tells me to take
off my shoes, because it's polite to, and she doesn't want
me to dirty her floors. But I refuse.

He observes me from behind his desk as if he misheard
me. I fold my arms defiantly, and he leans back in his chair.
"Ah," he says, nodding slowly, "this is what Pastor Brown
was talking about."

I don't know what he means. What did Pastor Brown tell him? What has he been saying behind my back? I can feel my throat closing. I try to remember what Rudy said, that they only win if you get mad, but I'm finding it hard to stay calm. So I count instead, because it's helped me a few times lately, so maybe I'm getting better at it.

"Why don't you sit down, Clara?"

I sit on a chair in front of his desk that reminds me of the school chairs, small and uncomfortable.

"Why won't you take off that thing on your head?" he asks.

"Why do I have to take it off?"

He takes a deep gulp of air. "Well, because I want to see Clara. Right now, Clara is hiding."

My lips purse tightly, and I clench my cheeks. "I'm not hiding. How can I hide? It's just a hat."

He sits forward. "Your parents are very worried about you. They tell me you are struggling to remember what happened last summer. That it is affecting your daily life. They think you might need some help."

Hot tears cloud my vision and I can no longer see him clearly. "What kind of help?"

He reaches into a side drawer and pulls out a Bible. He flicks through the pages, then stops. He passes the Bible to me.

"Proverbs three, verses five and six: read it."

I wipe my eyes so I can see the words. " 'Trust in the Lord with all your heart and lean not on your own understanding. In all your ways submit to him, and he will make your path straight.' "

Bishop Mason smiles. "Do you know what that means? It means that we, the church and your parents, we will guide you. We, through Jesus, will show you the right way. It will take some time, but we will get there. I have faith in you."

The Bible makes a thud on the ground as I spring to my feet. I yank the door open.

Mama and Papa jump when I appear in the hall. I run by them, along the corridor, and down the stairs. Behind me I hear Mama calling me, but all I want is to get as far away from them as possible.

I run blindly out of the building, pausing only to get my bearings. I don't know the city well enough to know where I am, but I know where the sea is. I stumble through the parking lot, pausing briefly at the roadside as cars whiz by. The traffic lights turn red, so I weave around cars to the other side. There is a small wall separating the walkway and the beach. It is low enough to climb, so I jump over it, landing feetfirst in the sand.

City sand is not like Sycamore sand. The grains feel like

small stones under my feet. It feels less welcoming, less like home. I take my shoes off, allowing my skin to feel the texture of the small stones. I look behind me, beyond the cars and the busy road. Papa and Mama are running across the parking lot. It's only sand, I tell myself, it won't harm you. It's the sea that can pull you under with no warning and no apology. I walk farther onto the beach. There are people dotted around, but none of them pay me any mind.

I sit down, sinking my toes deep into the sand, making imprints. My heart is beating so fast, I can barely breathe.

I notice a boy coming out of the water with a small surfboard. He is in a black wetsuit, excitedly talking to his father, his pale skin and floppy hair dripping from the water. The boy drops the surfboard on the beach and drags his father over to a man selling ice cream. My heart beats faster. I look out to sea, then back at the surfboard lying in the sand.

All I want is to get away. Just for a minute.

I hear Papa shouting my name. He is running down the sand toward me, his shoes in his hand. Before he can reach me, I am on my feet. I hear my breathing like thunder in my ears as I grab the kid's surfboard and run toward the sea.

Something stops me at the edge.

It is like there is an invisible barrier in front of me. I cannot go any farther. My feet won't let me. I start to gasp for breath and in my frustration throw the board in the sand and stomp on it.

I jump on the board over and over until it cracks under my feet. Screaming at the top of my lungs, I grab pieces in my hand, trying to break them even further. It is the voice of the boy's father that brings me back. He is running toward me. What's left of the board drops out of my hand as I realize what I have done.

"What is wrong with you? That's my son's."

I open my mouth to say something, but nothing comes out. The little boy bursts into tears while his father demands I pay for a new one.

Over all the commotion Papa reaches me, wrapping his arms around my shoulders. "It was a mistake," he tells the man, "she's going through some things." He pulls me closer, and I feel his heart beating almost as fast as mine. "How much for a new one?"

It is only then that I notice the crowd, all gathered together, pointing and shaking their heads. Maybe Bishop Mason was right; maybe there is something wrong with me.

CHAPTER
SEVENTEEN

OUR HOTEL IS ON A QUIET road about ten minutes from the beach. It sits between two office blocks and a patty warehouse. The bedrooms are behind a wired fence and surround a swimming pool that looks like it hasn't been cleaned since the hotel opened.

I lie on a crooked chair under broken umbrellas while Mama collects the keys for our room. The city isn't as fun as I expected. In fact, I can't wait to get home.

Papa is on the other side of the pool, pacing. First he was on the phone trying to get enough money to pay for the boy's surfboard. I feel awful and offer the little money I have saved from helping out at the only store on the hill.

Papa refuses it. He must have gotten the money, because

I hear him arrange to meet the father later. Then he is on the phone again, this time with Pastor Brown.

"You lied to us, Barry. You said he would help her. No, no, this is not helping her. This is the opposite of helping her."

He hangs up the phone, wiping his hands over his face. A pang of guilt overwhelms me as I watch Papa get so stressed. All because of me.

Mama calls me over with the keys in her hand.

The hotel room has two double beds and a brown dresser with an old TV. Mama tells me to get ready for bed right away. I don't argue. It's been a long day, and I'm exhausted.

When I finally pull the covers over me, Papa turns off the lights. I realize that I am not as tired as I thought I was. I am wide-awake. I squeeze my eyes as tight as I can because I so desperately want to forget about today.

Nothing happens. All I see is the backs of my eyelids. I open my eyes and stare for a while at the glimmer of moonlight seeping through a crack in the curtains. It is so bright, I guess it's probably a full moon. It might be fun to watch it outside. Much more fun than lying here listening to Papa snore.

Papa is lying on his back and Mama is snuggled under his arm. I tiptoe barefoot over to the door and open it slowly, wincing at the small creak it makes, but no one stirs.

I step outside and close the door gently behind me. It's late, but the air is still warm and heavy. It gives me no relief from the stuffy bedroom, which has only a broken fan in the corner of the room.

I go to the end of the walkway and turn the corner and pass more rooms. I go to the pool and sit on the side, dangling my feet into the murky water. I can't help remembering why I am here. Not because Mama and Papa wanted to take me on an adventure like they promised, but because they think I am going crazy.

"Clara?"

I open my eyes and Papa is standing beside me.

"Can't sleep?" he asks.

He sits and slips his bare feet into the pool, and we move our feet in circles under the warm water.

"You know your mother and I love you, right?"

I nod, staring hard into the pool at my wavy reflection.

"It hasn't been easy for any of us, but especially for you." He rubs his hands together, and even though it's not cold, he shivers. "Your mother and I have been trying to think of ways to get you to open up. We thought Bishop Mason could help." He shakes his head. "We were wrong. What we need to do is stop expecting other people to do what we should be doing."

I focus hard on my reflection so I don't cry. I'm sick of crying. I don't want to anymore.

"How about you and me go fishing?" he says. "I have a friend who can lend me his boat. It's been a while since I fished in these waters."

My body goes rigid. The thought of spending alone time with my father makes me happy. It's not something we ever do. But I don't know if I am ready to go back into the sea.

"But you said I wasn't to go into the water."

I feel his arms around me, and his loose twists prickle my skin. "I said you weren't to go into the water alone. Come, let's sneak off and have our own adventure. Just you and me. It's time, don't you think?"

CHAPTER
EIGHTEEN

WE WALK INTO TOWN JUST AS it is waking up. Workers dressed in blue, white, or khaki uniforms wait patiently for their buses to take them to work. The market men and women are unpacking the trunks of their cars. Papa calls out a hello to each one of them as we pass even though he knows none of them. That's just who he is. Papa talks to anyone. The market is a row of flimsy wooden huts on either side of the road, like the one in our town but much bigger. Pieces of wood overlap each other to make a roof as the market sellers prepare for the heat. The huts are open, with no doors, and the market men and women lay out tables for their food or just place the boxes on the ground.

Papa takes me through a small walkway between the

market huts and I smell the fresh sea air. He inhales and lets out a loud sigh. "Do you smell that?" he says. "That is the smell of happiness."

Our feet sink into the white sand, which pulls us down as we walk over to Papa's friend's boat. His friend keeps it tied up on the beach with four others. Papa tells me how many times he has told his friend to pay for someone to look after it, but his friend says everyone knows him and no one would take his boat. "This isn't Sycamore, where you can leave things lying around." Papa says. But maybe Papa's friend is right. Maybe no one will steal it. Of the five boats, his is the least likely to be taken. It is an old wooden boat that looks as though it would fall apart under a strong wave. Holes have been patched up, and the paint is peeling.

There is a life jacket in the boat, and Papa helps me into it. As he pulls it tight around me, I hear his breath and it is short and shallow. I try not to look at him because I think if I do, I might see something I don't want to see, and it will make me cry.

"Too tight?" he says as I wince. I shake my head and he asks me if I'm sure, because he can loosen it. But I can tell he doesn't want to loosen it, so I lie and say that it is fine.

I have been on a boat a few times, so I know what to do when Papa unties the rope and begins pushing the boat out to sea. This time, though, I stand at the edge of the water, watching him. Every time the small waves roll in, I take a step back. When Papa has taken the boat far enough off the sand, he jumps in and reaches for me, but I don't move.

"It only comes to your ankles," he assures me, like I don't know that already. I know I'm not going to drown in ankle-deep water, I know that, but my feet won't move. I am frozen to the spot and I don't know why. Papa gets out of the boat and makes his way back onto the shore. He lifts me up and carries me. "One step at a time, eh?"

He helps me into the boat and jumps in himself, taking the cord attached to my jacket and attaching it to the inside of the boat.

"You good?"

I nod, positioning myself in the middle of the boat. He moves to the back and starts the engine. I close my eyes tightly as we speed away from the shore. The water splashes over the sides, wetting our faces, and I can taste the sea salt.

We race through the sea, the small boat thrown up in the air with each wave. I close my eyes tighter and grit my teeth. When we are far enough out, Papa slows down and searches for a good spot. He tells me to look with him, but I don't move.

"Clara, look." He points to the water. I slide toward the

edge slowly, bit by bit, my hands shaking as I try to hold on to the wooden bench. I sit there for some time, willing myself to open my eyes and look into the sea. When I finally do, it is like glass; you can see right through it. Small fish swim around us, but none are worth our time. Papa continues to move around until he finally turns off the engine. "This is a good spot," he says.

I help him with a mesh box made with wires that will trap the fish. He places conch meat inside as bait to encourage the fish through the funnel-shaped opening, and we lower it into the sea on a rope so long, I am sure it must reach the ocean floor.

"Look at this," he says, indicating the entire view with a wave of his hands. "Tell me anywhere more beautiful than this." The boat gently rocks from side to side, but apart from the gentle lapping of the waves against us, the world is silent.

"So, you went to see Eldorath," Papa says, and I can feel his eyes on me.

"He's not a bad person," I say, staring hard at the bottom of the boat. "He's family and I don't understand why you would let family be treated that way."

Papa sighs. "You're right. He is family. But there are things about my brother you don't know. Things your mother and I, and Eldorath, agreed you shouldn't know."

I chance a squint in his direction. "Like what?" I wait for him to say what I have been hearing my whole life, that it doesn't matter what or why, I just need to listen and not go there.

"Just things" is all he says. "I used to be afraid of the water too, you know?" He doesn't wait for me to answer. "I don't know if I ever told you, but my father died in the sea. For a long time I was afraid of the water, like you, but then I decided the only way to tackle my fear was to face it head-on. You have to face it, Clara, or it will consume you like it did my brother."

I try to focus on what he is saying because I think he's trying to tell me why Eldorath doesn't leave his house, but I am distracted by the swaying of the boat, and the sound of the waves is giving me flashbacks. The calm sea, the dark sky, the heavy clouds, the shouting.

I force my eyes open. The ocean is so big, it could swallow me and Papa whole if it wanted. I look back at the shore and it is just a tiny speck. I nervously look over at Papa, who has that faraway gaze again.

The boat is getting smaller, and the ocean is getting bigger, and it feels as if we are being sucked down into the depths. I focus hard on my fingers circling lines that don't exist but keep me from looking my father in the eye.

"Clara, help me!" I look up and he is pulling at the

rope. Relief floods my face and I join him in pulling the rope up with what I hope is a good catch.

Papa gives his fish to the first fisherman he sees. The fisherman offers to pay, but Papa refuses to take his money. "Go sell them for a good price," Papa says. The fisherman then tells Papa to come to his restaurant, where he will make us a good breakfast. Papa never turns down a free meal, so we hurry back to the hotel to tell Mama.

Papa bursts into the hotel room, where Mama is still fast asleep. "Time to get up," he announces. "We have a free meal waiting for us."

Mama peers at him from under the covers, her eyes barely open. "Are you crazy? What time is it?"

Papa lets go of my hand and pulls the sheets off Mama. "Come on, woman, let's go before the sun rises."

The restaurant is about a ten-minute walk from where we are staying, and Mama complains the entire way.

"What in God's name has gotten into you, Lloyd? Have you lost your mind? It's too early for this."

But Papa only laughs.

When we get there, Papa greets the fisherman at the door,

and they exchange pleasantries. I can't hear what they're saying because Mama forces us to wait a few yards back, like we are going to catch something if we stand too close.

A few minutes later Papa waves us over, and I run to him, with Mama trailing hesitantly behind. Inside there are scatters of people still hanging on to the night. A few couples and four boys with skin pink from the sun dance in a circle, singing at the tops of their voices to a live band.

Mama takes my hand and moves me as far away from them as possible. She finds a table and plonks herself in a chair with such force, she almost topples over.

"What is he doing?" she mumbles, shaking her head in dismay. Papa disappears into the kitchen only to return minutes later with the same fisherman, who is now wearing a chef's hat and apron. Papa leads him to our table and introduces him to Mama.

"This is Oshiah, the fisherman we met this morning."

Mama goes to shake Oshiah's hand, but he hugs her instead.

"Have whatever you want from the menu," he says. "You just sit back and enjoy yourself."

Oshiah calls a waiter over to take our order and returns to the kitchen.

Meanwhile, Papa approaches the band, which is playing a Bob Marley song. The music ends, and the musicians exchange hugs. Papa takes a seat on the stage and is offered a guitar from one of the guys. His fingers move around the strings as he tunes it, and then, with a nod to the band, he starts playing.

Mama groans, shielding her face. "Everywhere we go he has to embarrass me."

I've only heard Papa play on his own. His audience is Mama, or me, but sometimes when he plays on the veranda, the neighbors come out to listen.

It's not just the way he plays, his fingers dancing along the strings, but it's his voice. Mama once said Papa's voice sounded like milk, and I hate milk, but I know what she means. It's thick and smooth. Every note he hits is perfect and soft. The room is dead quiet, and the boys on the dance floor are transfixed. I look over at Mama, and her sour face has softened. She wears a silly smile as she stares longingly at my father.

I look out onto the beach, and the sky is a beautiful orange and yellow. I watch in awe as the sun rises from the horizon, and the sea is a blanket of calm.

I start to count, but for a different reason this time. When I reach ten, I take a deep breath.

"Mama, can I go to the beach?"

Mama looks out to the sea. She nods reluctantly. "Okay, but I'm coming with you."

"Mama . . ."

But she will not hear it and promptly grabs my hand. We step out of the restaurant and onto the sand, stopping only to take our shoes off. Her grip tightens as we pause at the edge of the sand.

"Why now?" she asks gently. I look back at Papa through the opening of the glass doors, which have been pushed back to let in the sea breeze. He watches us carefully while he plays. I turn back to the sea as small ripples creep onto the sand.

"Papa said it's time. He said we have to face what we're afraid of or it will consume us."

She wraps her arm around my waist, looking up at the cloudless sky. "You know I never liked the water."

I smile. "I know."

She pulls me down into the sand, and we sit while Papa's voice soothes us. Mama puts her arm around my shoulder, and it is like a warm coat on a cold night.

"To me the sea was always this scary place. But you were different. You were fearless, like your father. You loved the ocean, and even though your father had bad memories of the sea, he never let on to you. He allowed you to explore the water for yourself. He didn't want you to be afraid, and you weren't. You fell in love with the water."

As she speaks, the sky turns black right in front of me,

the moon disappears, and I am running from the sea as fast as I can. My breath is stuck in my throat and I can't run fast enough, I can't catch my breath. I can't breathe. I squeeze my eyes as tight as I can, and when I open them, the sky isn't black anymore. All I can hear is Mama's frantic voice.

"Clara, what's the matter? Are you okay? Do you need water?"

It takes a while before my heart slows and my chest opens. I inhale, taking in the sea air. "I'm fine," I whisper, though my voice is croaky.

She kisses my forehead. "You were breathing so fast. What happened?"

I dig my toes into the sand and take a deep breath. "Mama, I'm starting to remember things."

Her brows are deep with worry. "What do you remember?"

I don't want to scare her. Or upset her even more than I have already.

"Just things," I whisper.

She pulls me tight. So tight, my body hurts, but I don't tell her because I know she needs this hug as much as me. "I love you so much," she whispers. "It will get easier, I promise." I don't know if she believes that or if she's just trying to make me feel better.

CHAPTER
NINETEEN

ON OUR WAY HOME MAMA AND Papa don't stop holding hands. Even when he needs to change gears or use the turn signals, he doesn't let go of her hand. It's as if our night in the city was really for them. During breakfast Mama glowed when the room erupted in applause for Papa. Now she can't stop looking at him with big wide eyes.

It was a good day for all of us. For me and Mama too.

The roads are busy today, even though we left later than usual to avoid the worst of the traffic. It hasn't worked. We are still bumper-to-bumper, barely moving through the city.

Mama points out two men carrying zinc panels on their heads, in front of them more people carrying planks of wood. Which could mean nothing, or for this island could mean something. Papa rolls down his window as we near them.

"What you building?" he calls to them.

"Not building," one of them answers back. "Protecting. Storm is coming."

Mama immediately turns on the radio. She spins the knob until we come to a station without static.

"—is expected to turn into a Category Five hurricane within the next twenty-four hours, with winds up to a hundred and eighty-five miles per hour. Residents are asked to stay home and off the roads. For those whose homes are near the water, an evacuation order has been issued."

There is a somber mood in the car. Papa leans his elbow on the door with a pained expression on his face. I look around and realize all the cars are packed with people's belongings. This is not work traffic; they are evacuating.

"Do you know a shortcut?" Papa asks Mama. His voice is heavy. Mama, who went to college in the city, looks around her to get her bearings. She used to joke to Papa that she knew every inch of the city because she had to walk everywhere.

"There is a left down there by the lights. You can come off the main road and take the hills, but, Lloyd, we're not moving anywhere for now." She's right; even if Mama knows the shortest and quickest way home, what use is it if we are stuck in a traffic jam?

Papa hits the steering wheel with an angry grunt. I feel my heart start to race and I don't know why. I have been through this plenty of times.

If you know anything about storms, you will know that everything stops just before everything goes crazy. You don't need to listen to the radio to know what's coming; you feel it. When we woke up earlier this morning, Papa opened the curtains and peered up at the sky. "Looks like storm," he mumbled. The sky was a dark gray, darker than when it is about to rain. When we got to the car, there was no wind, which seems pretty normal for the city, but the air wasn't heavy either. There was nothing. No air, no wind, no sun, just a sense of lingering. As if waiting for something.

When you live on a tropical island, you get to know these signs, but Mama and Papa didn't worry because they thought it was only a small storm, and small storms leave as quickly as they come. Mama reaches into the backseat and places her hand on my knee.

"You okay, baby?"

I nod, but I'm not. I feel something. It's in my chest, tightening, making it hard to breathe. It's as if I've been here before, in this moment. I wind down the window and stick my head out, inhaling the air, but there is nothing.

We sit in slow traffic for over an hour before Papa is able to turn off the main road and take the shortcut through the hills that Mama told him about.

As the car climbs the hill, leaving the traffic behind, Papa puts his foot down on the accelerator, and he doesn't take it off until we reach Sycamore.

The town is eerily quiet, like a ghost town. Shops are barricaded shut. The supermarket is the only place with people rushing in and out, piling bottles of water and canned food into their cars. Papa stops off in town and runs to the beach to secure his boat while me and Mama wait in the car.

When he comes back, he says his friend Milo had taken his boat into his boat shack along with his own.

When we reach Sycamore Hill, the air is filled with the sounds of hammers and saws as neighbors board up their houses.

Papa parks the car at the bottom of the hill, and even though we have the threat of a hurricane hanging over our heads, we are relieved to be home. He tells me to help Mama with our bags and walks the short distance to Pastor Brown's house to return the keys to the car.

Rudy is waiting for me on the embankment, and I don't know how long she's been there, but my heart skips when I see her. She throws her arms around my waist. "I've missed you, Clara." I can't deny it. I've missed her too.

"Go and get Ms. Gee, will you?" Mama says to us. "Bring her to the house."

"Mama, she won't come," I say.

She picks the bags up off the ground. "Then make her come, Clara," she snaps. "We don't have time for Ms. Gee's pride today." She climbs the hill, her arms full, leaving me to face the wrath of Ms. Gee.

I haven't spoken to Ms. Gee since we tried to steal her guava leaf, and even though she stood up for me at Mama's party, I still don't think she's happy with me.

Rudy and I are both silent for most of the walk. Rudy kicks stones. I can tell she has more than Ms. Gee on her mind.

"I bet she heard the car and is waiting with her cauldron," I say, trying to make her smile. It works; a small smile tips Rudy's lips.

I pull a naseberry leaf from Pastor Brown's tree and tear it in half. "This is the ointment we need to keep us from evil."

Rudy takes her piece and says, "What do we do with it?"

I rub it between my fingers, and she copies me. "If we rub it all over our skin, then nothing she says will affect us. We won't even get mad."

She chuckles, wiping the leaf on her arms and legs. "Will it protect us from the storm too?" she asks, and her voice is a whisper. I've never seen Rudy scared before. Now all I want to do is protect her.

"Hey."

I spin around to see Calvin leaning over his wall. "Your dad is pretty mad at my dad. What happened?" He jumps over the wall and runs to catch up with us.

I didn't even see him there on the veranda. I look behind him for his shadow, Gaynah, but she is not with him. I peer over at his house. "Papa?"

Calvin nods. "Something about Bishop Mason? I didn't stay to listen. So, what are you two up to?"

I rush past him and through his gate. "Where are you going?" he calls after me. I tiptoe up the steps to their veranda, and Papa's voice becomes clear as day. Through the window I see Papa with his back to me, and I wonder if he's forgotten there is a storm coming. He is pointing at Pastor Brown. "You betrayed us, Barry. You told us he would help her."

Pastor Brown steps toward Papa, his eyes bulging. "Betrayed you, Lloyd? I am a man of God. What I said to you was that girl needs help. I told you this the minute all the horror happened last year. But you didn't listen. Give her time, you said, let her figure herself out. She will come to her senses, you said. Now look at her. She is misbehaving. She is disobedient. She went to the house of hell, and still you did nothing. So what would you prefer me to do? To turn my back? To do nothing, like you?"

There is a long pause from Papa. All I see is his shoulders

rising and falling. He steps toward Pastor Brown. "That house of hell is my father's house. It's where you played as a child. We invited you to that house. You ate from our table. You slept in that house. Whatever feelings you have about my family, Barry, you will do well to remember that."

He turns to open the door, and I run down the steps and out the gate just as he comes out. Pastor Brown is right behind him. "Lloyd, don't let this split us. Rather, let it unite us. We are a community. We have fought this before; we will fight it again."

Papa spins round on his heels and shouts, "This is not our community, Barry. This is yours. It has always been yours."

He marches out the gate, stopping only when he sees me. His face is fiery, his mouth in a thin line. I've never seen Papa mad. Not ever.

"Clara, go and get my brother. Tell him storm is coming and he should be here, with us."

My heart skips a beat.

"But—but Mama told me to get Ms. Gee," I stammer.

He shakes his head, heading toward us. He throws a defiant look at Pastor Brown. "I'll get Ms. Gee. You get my brother. Be quick. Storm is almost here."

CHAPTER
TWENTY

ELDORATH HASN'T BOARDED UP ANY OF his windows like everyone else on the hill has. I think that might be because he doesn't have a ladder tall enough to reach them. But he does have these green wooden shutters, which are firmly closed.

Gaynah has followed me up the hill. I am surprised she wanted to go anywhere with me, but I guess she didn't want to miss the excitement of bringing Eldorath back to the village. Rudy and Calvin wanted to come too, but Papa took Rudy with him to get her mother and Ms. Gee, and Pastor Brown ordered Calvin into the house.

So now it was just me and Gaynah. I'm hoping we get this over and done with quickly so Gaynah and I don't have to spend much time together.

It takes a few bangs on the door before Eldorath opens. He peers out through a crack of the door. "What in goodness gracious are you doing here?"

"Papa told me to come and get you," I tell him proudly. "He wants you to be with us for the storm."

A look of warmth flits across his face, but it changes quickly. "That's not possible. If certain people saw me, there would be a riot. Now go home." He shoos us away and shuts the door.

Gaynah turns to me. "Now what?"

I stare at the closed door, then at the ever-looming storm in the sky. A rumble of thunder explodes in the sky, reminding us the storm is not far away. *Make sure you're home after the first thunder,* Papa always says. *The storm could be another hour, or it could be another minute.*

We could make it home before the storm if we ran. We might catch the beginning of the rain if we left now. But Papa asked me to get Eldorath, and I won't leave without him. My gut clenches, and I slide to the porch floor. "We wait," I tell her.

We sit on Eldorath's porch, waiting for him to change his mind and open, but he doesn't. Gaynah starts to regret following me up here. "Mama will be worried," she says. "I'm supposed to be home before the storm comes. She's going to be mad." When I don't answer, she glares at me. "She'll blame you." I lean against the door and my stomach gets tighter. She's right. This will be another excuse for Juliette to say I am leading her daughter astray.

"You go," I say, staring blankly into the forest. "If you leave now, you might get back before the storm."

Gaynah looks doubtfully at the sky. "Do you think so?"

As if to answer her question, the sky opens, and the rain comes. Only it's not gentle; it's a downpour. We have some shelter under Eldorath's door, but not much. When the wind starts, we will not stand a chance. We simultaneously bang on Eldorath's door as hard as we can, screaming at him to open up.

Usually when the storm comes, we are already indoors. If the rain doesn't start too heavy, we might sit outside on the veranda and watch. I love storms. Sometimes I'll run out into the rain with Papa. We'll stand in the middle of the front yard and let it pour down on us. Gaynah hates storms. She especially hates thunder. I see her grimace as another one crashes overhead. We may not be friends right now, but I don't want her to be afraid.

I thump my fist against the door. "Let us in!"

Eldorath doesn't answer. I thought he would open the door once the rain started. But whatever Sycamore has done, it has scared him, and he does not want us in his house.

I am about to give up when the door opens and we fall

in. I look up and Eldorath is looking down at us. "Come in before you catch a cold," he says, hurrying us in. We stumble to our feet and gratefully step inside. He peers out into the rain as if he is looking for someone, I don't know who. "Well, you can't go home in that," he says. Quickly he shuts the door and bolts it.

Eldorath gives us a room to change out of our damp clothes. "There should be plenty of clothes in there," he says, pointing to a large oak wardrobe leaning against a fabric wall. "Call me if you need anything."

As he leaves, the door creaks shut behind him and we are plunged into near darkness. A four-poster bed fills the space, its dark wood making the room even darker, with flowery curtains pulled back against the frame.

It is silent apart from the rain pouring down outside. Gaynah moves over to the window, her arms wrapped against her stomach. This is the first time we have been alone since the game. So much time has passed since our fight, and now it seems more normal to not speak than to break the silence.

I open the wooden wardrobe against the wall and run my fingers through rows of clothes similar to the ones in Eldorath's room.

I hold up a silver jumpsuit from the eighties and wave it around. "This would suit you."

Gaynah half turns, her arms still folded firmly around her stomach. She raises an eyebrow comically. "Really?"

I frown a little, looking at the jumpsuit. "What's wrong with it? It's sparkly, and you like sparkly things."

She rolls her eyes. "You really don't know me, do you, Clara. I would never touch any of this cheap stuff."

For a second I get ready to tell her that I know her better than anyone. Sometimes better than herself. I know that she sucks her thumb when she's nervous, and snaps at people when she's scared. I also know that my uncle's clothes are not cheap. They're more expensive than anything she ever wears. Instead, I clamp my mouth shut and try to count.

I reach ten and feel my shoulders relax. I don't want to be mad at Gaynah anymore. It's tiring being this mad all the time, and I miss her.

"You look, then," I say. "I'm going to find Eldorath." And I leave the room, still in my wet clothes.

I walk along the hall and turn the knob of the first door I come to. It's another bedroom. I close it and continue to the next door. I open it: a closet with towels and bathroom supplies. At the end of the hall is the room where we first saw Eldorath's costumes, when Rudy was so excited to play dress-up.

The wind howls around the house, and there is a cold

gust in the room. I shiver, following the hall as it wraps around the stairs. Eldorath stands framed against a large tinted window. I hesitate to approach him, but it's as if he senses me, and he turns. "Clara." His face is covered by the shadow of the curtain, his hands clasped in front of him. "Is everything okay?"

I nod, noting how haunting he looks against the window. He walks toward me, and as he reaches me, he whispers, "Come, I have something to share with you."

I follow him hesitantly as he leads me into the room filled with clothes we visited the first day. Behind the rows of clothes is a door that leads into another room, much smaller than the one before. It has a desk with a chair behind it, and another chair in front of it. He sits behind the desk and fiddles with a pen shaped like a snake. "This is my office," he explains, waving his hand around at the empty room. "I keep meaning to decorate it, but I just can't find the time"—he sighs—"or the inclination." He leans back in the chair, observing me from under his bushy eyebrows.

"Can you keep a secret, Clara?"

I think about this because I don't want to lie. Maybe I can keep a secret, but what if the secret is bad? Eldorath waits patiently while I weigh the pros and cons of answering his question. If I say no, then I'll never know what his secret is. If I say yes, something bad might happen.

"Okay, I'll tell you," Eldorath says, sitting forward.

"No, no, no. I don't want to be trapped in here forever because of your secret."

He squints at me, confused. "You won't be trapped here, Clara. You can leave anytime you choose."

It's a trap.

"It's not a trap," he says, as if reading my mind. Oh God, he reads minds too? This is more than I ever imagined. I knew he wasn't a witch doctor, but a mind reader? Think of something else. Mango. Think of mango. If he says anything about mangos, then that means he knew everything I was thinking this whole time. Even the bad thoughts. I bite my lip.

I wait.

We look at each other, waiting for the other to speak.

Eldorath sighs, "What are you doing now?"

"Seeing if you can read my mind."

"I can't."

"Are you sure?"

"Yes, I'm sure."

I sigh with relief. "Okay, so what's your secret?"

He looks so intently at me, I shift my feet from side to side. "I used to see things, things that most people don't see," he says.

My chest rises and falls as I think about the rumors.

The stories. Is this it? Is this when I find out if the rumors are true?

"What do you mean?" I breathe.

Eldorath leans forward in his chair, resting his elbows on the desk.

"Clara, I am just like you. I can see dead people too."

I turn on my heels and run along the landing. Behind me I hear Eldorath calling me back, telling me it's okay, there's nothing to be afraid of, but I continue running along the landing and down the stairs. When I can no longer hear him, I slow down, gasping for breath. I stumble to the glass door, where the heavy rain fills his balcony. My heart is beating superfast and my head feels like it's going to explode.

I don't know what he means. I'm afraid to know and I don't know why. Maybe I'm afraid of being like him. Maybe I knew all along but didn't want to admit it.

I hear footsteps behind me and groan inwardly.

"I love rain, don't you?" he says, approaching me.

I do love the rain, but it's hard to focus when I don't know what he is going to ask me next. Suddenly I wish I hadn't come here. My gut feels uneasy and my mind is screaming for him to not say anything else. I stare hard at the pellets of rain hitting the veranda outside.

"The community loved my father. He was a loud,

friendly man who lived in the big house on the hill. Pastor Brown, your father, your mother, we were all inseparable. This house was our playground." He trails off. "My father loved to fish; it's where your father gets it from. He often took us with him—me, your father, Barry. He would teach us what to do, tell us the names of each fish, show us how to find the right spot. One Sunday morning he wanted to go fishing, but I was the only one awake, so we decided to go alone. As we were leaving, Moses, Pastor Brown's father, showed up. He usually never went anywhere with us, but for some reason he turned up at my father's door and said he wanted to come too. He'd had a dream the night before that something significant happened on water. He thought God was speaking to him. I wanted to wake Barry, because his father rarely ever did anything with him. Barry spent so much time at our home, he became like family. But Moses said no, let him sleep."

He moves around me so we are facing each other, and this time I don't run. I stay to listen. This is the story I've wanted to know my whole life. The truth.

He sighs heavily, and he is trembling a little.

"The water was choppy when we arrived, and Moses said he didn't like the look of it, but my father insisted—he had made these journeys a hundred times, in worse weather, and he had been fine. It was obvious from the get-go it wasn't fine, but my father was a stubborn man, and he continued to take us farther out. The rain came and it was torrential, and the waves got bigger." He lowers his head. "Our boat was too small. It couldn't handle the waves, and so it capsized."

I inhale sharply.

"We went under, all of us: Papa, me, Moses. The water was cold. It took my breath away. I remember falling farther and farther down until a hand grabbed me out of nowhere and pulled me up. My father saved me, threw me on top of the overturned boat, and told me to hold on tight. *Don't let go,* he said. Then he went back under for Moses. I waited for what seemed like hours, in the wind and rain, holding on for my life. But they never came. It was hours later before a rescue boat found me, just me."

I swallow the lump in my throat.

"That same night, I saw them both in my room, telling me it was time to go fishing as though it'd never happened. When I told Barry that I'd seen his father, he didn't believe me. He said his father was in the city, and he would know if he had come to Sycamore. He thought I was lying until the funeral, then he got mad and he stayed mad. Our relationship has not been the same since. He blamed me for his father's death. He wished I had woken him that day, but more than that, I think when I told him I saw his father after he died, he saw that as the ultimate betrayal, that even in his death, his father still hadn't come to him."

Eldorath smiles weakly, shaking his head. "Ever since then he's been on a campaign to ruin me. He took over his father's ministry and continued the campaign against me, until finally I gave up. I stopped going out. The stares, the whispers, the rumors got to be too much. Your father tried many times to draw me out of this house. To this day he knocks on my door with a basket of food and invites me to dinner. But why would I want to eat with a community that hates me? I would rather stay here, alone, with my own company."

My heart feels heavy. I feel so sad for Eldorath in that moment and so mad at myself for wanting to leave. All this time, all the rumors were because Pastor Brown was still hurt by his own father's death, and he's been taking it out on Eldorath.

Eldorath moves me into the sitting room across from the piano room. This room is more lived-in, but cobwebs still hang from the chandeliers, and I wonder if it's because he can't reach them. A painting of a man stands tall on the wall in front of us. It must be Grandpa, even though I never met him.

Eldorath sits me down on a sofa with pink and white roses stitched into the cover. He takes my hand in his, and it's warm and soft like sheets after they've been washed. He smells of coconut oil. I never noticed that before.

"Clara, your father doesn't allow you up here because he doesn't want to admit you are going through the same thing as me. He got into many fights and arguments protecting me over the years. He saw the damage that fear could do. He thinks if he keeps you away, you'll get better, and no one will ever have to know you see ghosts too."

My lip trembles as I try to hold myself together. I think about all the rumors I have heard about Eldorath. All the times Mama has told me not to go to his house. All the times I've asked Papa if I could go with him and he told me, *Another time.*

"I'm like you?" I whisper, and the question comes out in a gush of breath that stings my throat. Eldorath smiles and nods.

I can barely look at him. "How do you know?"

"Remember I said I was going to help you?" he says. "That time is now, Clara." He nods upstairs.

"So tell me what happened to Gaynah. How did she die?"

CHAPTER
TWENTY-ONE

BEFORE

THERE IS A NEW GIRL ARRIVING in Sycamore. Her hair is in two Afro buns with big white bows, and she is wearing cat's-eye sunglasses, like a celebrity. That's according to Gaynah. I haven't seen her yet, but Gaynah says she saw her get off the city bus by the traffic circle with a woman that looked like her mother, and they are heading up the hill.

But Gaynah says a lot of things. She said she saw an alien once down by Ms. Gee's guava tree. The alien had eight legs and three eyes and told her not to tell anyone because humans might hurt her. Of course, Gaynah being Gaynah, she told everyone she saw.

While we wait on the grass by the turn of the road, Calvin suggests we think of ideas to do with the new girl, places we can show her. I suggest Fort Charlotte, an old fort by the sea with cannons left over from the war. Calvin agrees this is a good call, but Gaynah shuts it down immediately.

"We're not playing make-believe," she retorts. "That's for babies, Clara. Are you a baby?"

"We don't need to call anyone names," Calvin says, intervening. "Let's just come to an agreement." This doesn't make Gaynah happy. She turns her back on me, rolling her eyes. Gaynah has been doing this a lot lately, embarrassing me in front of everyone. For some reason, she doesn't like our friendship anymore. She's never told me why. There are only six kids on the hill, plus three babies: the Wilson twins, Anton, Calvin; Gaynah; and me. There are a few older kids, like Anton's brother, but they do their own thing and are hardly ever on the hill. I have no one but Gaynah, so if Gaynah is going to ditch me for Calvin's group, I need this new girl.

Turns out Gaynah wasn't lying. The new girl is real, and she's everything Gaynah described. Rudy is her name. She came from New York to stay with Ms. Gee for the summer.

We're supposed to play pick leaf tomorrow, but the excitement of having someone new in Sycamore takes over. We agree to postpone the game for another day. Today we will show her the best of what Sycamore has to offer.

Which isn't much. Gaynah pouts and makes a fuss until my Fort Charlotte idea gets outvoted for the beach. Everyone loves the beach, even Gaynah.

The Wilson twins can't make it, they have track practice, and for once Anton isn't attached to Calvin's hip—he has chores to do and can't make it either. In the end it is just me, Gaynah, Calvin, the new girl, and the new girl's mother.

We walk the ten minutes down to the coast with Rudy stopping every few minutes to squeal at the cute roads and the cute houses and so many trees. After a while we get weary of the constant stopping in the scorching heat. Only Gaynah had the common sense to wear a hat. She lets us know this every time someone moans how hot it is.

By the time we get there, the sea is so welcoming, we run fully clothed into the crystal clear water. The new girl squeals as she enters the sea. She tells us she has never been to the beach and she can't believe how warm the water is. She splashes us, which then breaks into a water fight. Gaynah doesn't get involved. She sits on the sand under her hat and sunglasses, pretending she doesn't care to join, but I know she does.

Rudy's mother has found a shaded spot to read her book and barely pays us any mind except to tell us not to swim out too far.

Rudy whispers that we should sneak up on Gaynah and

drag her into the water. That's when I know I like her. Not many people mess with Gaynah; she has this snotty attitude because her mother is the head of our school. I am the only one brave enough to push her buttons because we are family and we are best friends. She forgives me sooner or later. The new girl doesn't know that about Gaynah yet, but I admire her bravery. The sun goes in and is replaced by a dark cloud. This doesn't faze us; it might rain for a few minutes, but then the sun will reappear as if nothing happened.

Rudy sits next to Gaynah in the sand and does exactly as I instruct her: she takes an interest in Gaynah's bag. Gaynah falls for it, of course, while me and Calvin sneak up on her from behind. Before she knows what's going on, I grab her arms, and Calvin grabs her legs. We drag her kicking and screaming across the hot sand and dump her in the water. She goes under, then comes up spluttering and screaming. Her bag is ruined. We forgot to take the bag off her. She is furious and lunges at me.

"I'm sorry," I shout, ducking her flying hands. I can't help but laugh because she looks so funny snarling at me with her hair and clothes soaking wet. All the things she takes pride in.

"Now, that's not very nice, is it?" Rudy's mom calls from under her shade, but she doesn't move to stop us.

She's too busy fanning herself and gulping down a bottle of water.

Calvin gets away from Gaynah by swimming out of reach, but she's not mad at him; she's mad at me. My laughing turns to frustration that I am the only one she's angry at. We begin to argue. She demands that I buy her a new bag.

"Okay," I say dryly, "let me just get on my private jet and fly to America." I pretend to climb into a plane and buckle myself in. This infuriates her even more. So I dive into the water and swim away, knowing Gaynah doesn't like to go too far out.

But she doesn't give up that easy when she's mad at you. She follows me along the sand, screaming, "I hate you, Clara!"

The entire sky is black now. A normal sunny afternoon now looks like a stormy evening. Out of the corner of my eye I see Papa returning with his boat, which is unusual because he normally stays out longer. He is waving and shouting something, but I can't hear what he's saying, so I wave back.

I continue to swim, now toward the rock face, to get to the beach on the other side of the rock. I want to get as far away from Gaynah as possible. This side of the beach is known for its strong currents. Surfers are here every day to ride these waves. Today, though, it's empty because the sea is calm. Not just calm, it's flat; there are no waves, not even a ripple. It's weird, and for a second, I stop swimming and check the sky.

Maybe that is more than just a rain cloud; maybe it's a storm. There were no warnings on the radio this morning. Mama always has the radio on when she's making break-fast. Papa didn't say anything about a storm either. If there was even a slight threat, he would not have left this morn-ing except to secure his boat.

I hear Gaynah and turn to see her swimming toward me. "Really?" I shout. Was she that mad at me that she would get back in the water and chase me down? Gaynah is not one for deep water—she likes to be able to touch the ground—but we are just far enough out for the sandy bot-tom to be out of reach.

She's gasping when she catches up with me, and strug-gling to talk and stay afloat. "Your father . . . says . . . a storm's coming. . . . The current is too strong round here. You have to come back." I look over her shoulder, and Papa is running into the water, waving his arms. I look toward the rocks. I am nearly there.

I tell Gaynah to go back, but she shakes her head. "You're not strong enough!" I scream at her.

Her face screws up as she treads water. "You're not bet-ter than me, Clara. I can swim just as well as you."

"Fine," I shout. "Do what you want."

I swim as fast as I can around the rock because I know once she sees how deep it is, she will turn back. Out of the corner of my eye I see her pass me. She disappears around the rock, and I hear her scream before I see her. She is pulled into a whirlpool and is desperately trying to swim out, only to be pulled back in.

I am frozen. I can't move forward, and I can't move backward. I don't know what to do. The whirlpool appeared out of nowhere. I have never seen anything like it. My feet paddle frantically underwater.

I have to help her. She's not a strong swimmer; she can't get out by herself. I stretch my arm out to swim toward her when I am grabbed from behind. It's Papa.

"No." He grabs me, kicking and screaming, turning me onto my back. "People are coming," he says into my ear. "People are coming."

He drags me away as a group of people gathers on top of the rocks and a rope is thrown down. I find out later it was too late. They didn't get to her in time.

Every day after the accident, I would wake to find Gaynah sitting at the edge of my bed. She was like the Gaynah I remembered. Her hair was long and straight. Every day she would say the same thing: "Come on, you can't sleep forever." I would pull the covers over my head and not move until I was sure she was gone.

One day, I woke up to see Gaynah's long eyelashes blinking at me. Her bag was safe across her chest.

"Get up, lazy. There's a new girl coming today."

It was as if nothing had happened. I was living the day all over again. Only this time, we would not go to the beach. This time, we would avoid the beach at all costs. It would be just as I wanted it. The new girl would be my new friend. I would take her to the fort and the river, and maybe to the city if we're lucky. I will show her the banana grove and my secret hideout. It would be the summer I wanted but never got.

My face is wet with tears and my throat feels like stones are inside. "I think I must have wanted the summer we were meant to have. But things were different. Gaynah hated me, it was like she blamed me for everything."

Eldorath waits patiently for me to finish. "Gaynah isn't mad at you," he says softly. "You are mad at yourself. She is here because you can't let her go. The arguments, the adventures, everything you have done is all you. This is what you wanted. Clara. You are controlling all this."

I think about the river and Gaynah laughing at me. I think about her revealing my secret dugout. Gaynah didn't do any of those things when she was alive. Sure, she said some mean things, and she treated me pretty badly for a best friend, but the river, the dugout, I made that up. I needed a reason to be mad at Gaynah. Maybe I haven't forgiven her for the argument on the beach because that's how it all started.

"What happens now?"

When he doesn't answer, I look up and he is a blur. "I've made peace with my ghosts a long time ago. Now, dear Clara, it's time for you to make peace with yours."

TWENTY-TWO

WHEN I ENTER THE ROOM, GAYNAH looks up angrily. "Where have you been? I thought you left me and went home. I looked everywhere for you."

I collapse onto the bed to stop my legs from shaking.

She stands above me, glaring down. "Well? Where have you been? And how are you going to explain this to my mama, because she's going to be mad at you for bringing me here."

I stare at the carpet with its swirly lines and white dots. "I didn't bring you here. You followed me," I say quietly.

"No, I didn't. You brought me here."

I realize she's right. I did bring her here. I bring her everywhere. Make peace with your past, Eldorath said, so I raise my eyes to meet hers.

"Why do you hate me so much?" The words tumble out in a river of pain, and my voice cracks under the strain.

Gaynah's eyes widen. "Why do I hate you? Why do you hate me?"

I fumble over my words, completely confused. "What? Why do you think I hate you?"

"Because you left me, knowing full well I couldn't swim."

I lose my breath and sink to the floor. The room closes in. I cover my head with my hands to block out the thoughts of that day, but they still seep in, forcing their way through the cracks. I must be screaming, because Eldorath rushes in. He gets down on the floor next to me, saying words I can't hear.

After some soothing, the clouds slowly clear.

"Clara, remember what I said. It's all in your head," he says, peering under my arm so I can see him. "She's only saying what you're thinking. Remember, you're keeping her here. It's your story she's reliving. There were so many questions I asked myself when I realized I was seeing the ghost of my father. What was I blaming myself for? Why couldn't I let go? And the truth is, there is nothing I could have done, just as there is nothing you could have done. If you want it to stop, then you must first stop blaming yourself."

I'm not convinced. There are so many things I could

have done to stop her from swimming to that rock. I knew the waves could be powerful around there. Just because it looked calm didn't mean it was. Papa told me all the time to never take the sea for granted. *Always be prepared,* he said. *It can change at any second.* I failed him. I failed Gaynah.

I wipe the tears away, but they come back just as quickly. "I should have told you not to swim over there, Gaynah. I'm sorry." I see her take a breath. Her shoulders go limp and she turns. We look at each other for what seems like the first time, and I feel a deep sadness for her that I cannot describe.

I wish I had told her I was sorry at the beach.

None of this would have happened if I had just said sorry.

I'm woken by someone shaking my arm When I open my eyes, Mama is standing over me, her eyes filled with worry. I rub my eyes and look around. It takes me some time to remember I am in Eldorath's house. Mama points a flashlight at my face and I squint in its glare. She tells me to get up. I turn to wake Gaynah, but she is gone.

"Is the storm over?"

Mama grabs me by the arm and leads me out of the bedroom, where Papa is waiting on the landing.

"Is the storm over, she says." She repeats my words to Papa, who asks me if I am okay. They usher me down the stairs in the pitch-black, and I wonder if they sneaked in without telling Eldorath, because none of the lights are on.

It's only when we reach the front door that I see him hovering in the darkness, a gown wrapped tightly around him. The electricity must have gone, because Eldorath has a flashlight too.

"Thank you for looking after her," Papa says, hugging his brother firmly. "We tried to get here sooner, but the storm wasn't letting us."

"Don't be too hard on her," Eldorath says, nodding to me. "She's special."

Papa glances down at me and agrees, pulling me closer. Then he says, "Will you come with us?"

I look up at Eldorath with pleading eyes, but he shakes his head, forcing a smile. "Not today," he says quietly.

Papa opens the front door, and the howling wind rushes in as though it has been waiting for us. "You'll come and see us soon?" Papa asks Eldorath, and I can tell it's not the first time he's asked, because he doesn't wait for Eldorath to answer.

Papa turns to face the rain, wraps a towel over my head, and pulls me to him, bracing me for the outside.

"Ready?" he shouts to Mama over the noise of the storm.

"She's gone," I choke.

Papa looks down at me. "Who?"

"Gaynah."

They both exchange that look I have seen so many times. The look that says they know Gaynah has been gone for some time.

Papa squeezes me closer and kisses my forehead. "Let's get you home."

Pastor Brown is waiting in his car on the narrow road that leads back to our village. He is watching a wavering tree nervously when Papa opens the door, and we jump in. Juliette is in the front seat next to Pastor Brown, while me, Mama, and Papa squeeze into the back. Juliette turns, scowling at me.

"Not now, Juliette," Mama warns.

Juliette faces forward again. "That girl will be the death of us all," she mumbles.

I scowl at the back of her head. No one asked her to come out in the storm. The car rocks from side to side on the stony road. The wind and rain are the only sounds we hear for the rest of the journey home.

Rudy is fast asleep in my bed, so Papa must have convinced Ms. Gee to stay. I slip under the sheets, being careful not to wake her. Mama tucks me into bed like a baby, while Papa waits for her by the curtains. Mama kneels on the floor and strokes my face.

"I didn't mean to worry everyone," I whisper, because I want her to know I'm not a bad person like Pastor Brown suggests. "We—I just got trapped in the storm."

She nods. "I know, baby, but you know how special you are to us."

She kisses me on the forehead, then joins Papa at the door.

"Mama," I whisper before they leave, "is this why you didn't want me to go to Eldorath's house?"

"What do you mean, baby?" she says. Papa lays a hand on her shoulder.

"Because he knew that I saw Gaynah."

Papa smiles. "It's all good now, though, right?"

I nod because it is, but it doesn't answer my question. They leave, pulling the curtain behind them.

Outside I hear their lowered tones. Pastor Brown, Juliette, Mama, and Papa. Eventually they say their good-byes, and the front door closes.

CHAPTER
TWENTY-THREE

THE NEXT MORNING, MAMA IS THE first one outside assessing the damage. Her loud gasps wake me. I join her, Ms. Gee, and Papa outside. Rudy is a few seconds behind me, and so is her mom, barefoot in a head tie and nightie. Ms. Gee demands to know what Mama sees, so Mama describes what is in front of her.

The roof is the worst of our damage. The zinc roof over the kitchen is completely gone. Mama and Papa tried to give it a temporary fix last night while we all slept. The mango tree was completely blown over and is now leaning against the house. The yard is sprayed with telephone lines, a chicken pen from someone's house, and a random chair. Branches are everywhere.

Slowly people emerge from their houses. There is a silence that only implodes with cries of dismay as something else is discovered. From our yard I can see that Gaynah's house is damaged. Her roof, just like ours, has taken a major hit. Ms. Gee demands we guide her back to her house. No one argues because we are as desperate to see as she is. Still in our nightclothes, we make the slow, painstaking journey down the hill, stepping over zinc panels, branches, and fallen trees.

I feel Rudy brush beside me. She slips her hand into mine, gripping me tightly.

Water streams down the hill like a river, bringing rubble and branches with it. We pass Pastor Brown's house, and his wall is damaged, his roof in the same state as everyone else's. Ms. Gee is unusually quiet. She doesn't ask for any more updates, but that's maybe because she can tell from our silence it is not good.

When we reach her yard, she lets go of Papa's arm, then feels her way across the garden to the steps to her house. Papa rushes over and grabs her, but she fights him off. She feels in front of her frantically.

"Where is it? Where's my house?"

No one wants to be the one to tell her. There is nothing left but the steps.

Ms. Gee's house is a crumbled heap on the ground.

Broken wood and furniture litter her yard. We knew of all the houses to be hit the worst, it would be hers.

All her belongings are scattered around the yard. Her mattress is stuck in a bush, her dining table in bits. She has lost everything, even her rocking chair, the one she sat in every day. Ms. Gee collapses on the steps, wailing, her voice echoing over the hill.

Her screams bring everyone running. Not just Pastor Brown and Calvin, who live around the corner. Everyone. Sometimes one at a time, sometimes more; some dressed, others still, like us, in their nightclothes. Within minutes Ms. Gee's yard is filled with neighbors all surveying the scene in utter dismay.

Ms. Gee has always been part of Sycamore Hill. Ever since I was born. Ever since Mama was born. Everyone knows Ms. Gee as the mean old lady, but they say it with fondness. They roll their eyes when they hear her yelling and chuckle when they see me running. They talk among themselves about how her face is so mean, it's going to stick that way.

Ms. Gee is the real head of our hill. If you know Sycamore Hill, you know Ms. Gee. The kids are frightened of her, but no one hates her. She is just miserable Ms. Gee. So with her house destroyed, it is as if our own houses were destroyed. Her tears are our tears, because Ms. Gee never cries.

People begin to pick up pieces of her house and place them in piles. Someone finds a broom, someone else pulls her mattress from the bush. Rudy and her mom sit on either side of Ms. Gee and do not leave her.

I roam among the rubble, collecting items I know Ms. Gee will not want to lose. Her Bible from the tree branches and pieces of wood. A gold necklace with a cross, sticking out of the dirt. I bend down, brushing away the dirt and rubble to find a bunch of letters neatly packed together with a ribbon. The envelopes are soaking wet, but I recognize the ink stamp on the top right-hand side of the letters: New York.

I look around for Calvin and find him gathering branches to make a pile. I thrust the letters under his nose. He peers at it. "What is it?"

I wait until he throws the branches on a pile and walks over to me, taking the letters out of my hand.

"You've never seen them before?"

He frowns, flicking through the white envelopes. "No."

"Ms. Gee never asked you to read them to her?"

He shakes his head, handing them back to me.

"What about Anton? Or the twins?"

"Don't you think we would know if they read letters from New York?" he says, piling more branches into his arms. "Nothing happens around here, remember?"

I look over at Rudy and her mom. So if none of us

167

collected Ms. Gee's letters and read them to her, then who did?

Papa stands on the steps and asks for everyone's attention.

"This is a terrible thing for all of us," he says somberly. "This is our community. When one of us suffers, we all suffer. When one of our houses is gone, it feels like all our houses are gone. I know you all want to help, so let us do this the right way. Let us go home, get dressed, have some food, and meet back here in a few hours. There is a lot to do, but let us start here."

Everyone agrees and returns to their own homes.

CHAPTER
TWENTY-FOUR

FOR THE NEXT WEEK, THE HILL gets busy cleaning up after the storm. Papa organizes everyone to start at Ms. Gee's house, the worst hit. We work in the intense heat, collecting pieces of wood that used to be Ms. Gee's house and placing them in a pile.

Pastor Brown offers to go into town to get bottles of water to keep us going, but I think he just doesn't want to work in the sun.

I don't see Gaynah and assume she has gone. I can't help but feel a sense of loss all over again. She was my best friend. I miss our adventures. Even the sad ones down at the river. Even the arguments. I miss them all.

Amber Wilson scoops handfuls of leaves from the

ground, making a pile. She glances at me from under her long eyelashes. "It was me," she says quietly.

I look up at her blankly.

"I told Anton about your hideout."

I stand, placing my arms firmly on my hips, and glare at her.

"I can see the back of your house from the coconut tree in our yard. I go there sometimes to think. Training for re-lays gets to be a lot sometimes and, you know, parents. The pressure is a lot, you know?" She pauses. "I was there when you ran in by yourself. I saw you take those mangos from the ground and hide in there. I told Calvin and Anton, but I didn't think they were going to say anything. I thought it was cool you had somewhere to go and hide. I wish I had somewhere like that."

I think back to that day at the river when Anton made fun of me. When I blamed Gaynah before I knew Gaynah wasn't real.

"It was you," I say quietly, almost relieved. After I knew Gaynah wasn't real, I started to think I had made those things up, that they weren't real either. I nod slowly. "Okay."

"You're not mad?" she asks.

And I realize I'm not. Before, I would have been mad, but something has changed in me. I have made peace with my past and no longer feel angry. "No," I say, and I walk away. Amber and I will never be close friends, but maybe if I go to my hideout, I will look for her in the tree, and maybe, just maybe, if I feel like it, I might invite her down.

Collecting all the wood takes a full day. After we have all the wood in one pile, we sort out what can be reused.

Ms. Gee refuses to build a new house from brick like the rest of us, and I can tell Papa is frustrated that we might be doing this all over again after the next storm.

On the second day, around late afternoon, Rudy and I are busy sweeping the leaves in the yard, when the normal chatter and laughter around me stops.

I look around, and everyone is staring toward the entrance of Ms. Gee's yard. It's Eldorath, dressed in his usual purple suit, even on this hot day. Rudy squeals and runs over to him. My heart beats fast and I run to him, wrapping my arms around his waist. I hear his relief as he hugs us back.

"Was this a bad idea?" he asks me through a fixed smile. I shake my head, knowing deep down this might not go well. This is the first time anyone has seen Eldorath at a gathering for years. Calvin shakes his hand, but Eldorath pulls him into a tight hug. It's as if we have all been through something special together, something no one else could understand. Even if the village doesn't accept Eldorath, at least he has us now.

Papa approaches us and shakes Eldorath's hand. "Thanks for coming, brother," he says, and his voice is a little shaky as they hold on to each other for a little longer than normal. "You here to help?"

Eldorath looks behind Papa at the staring crowd. "Yes, if you want me to?" It is more of a question whether Papa wants him there, and I wait anxiously for Papa to do the right thing.

Papa turns to the curious faces and points to a pile of wood. "We're sorting out the good wood from the bad." Papa glances at Eldorath's attire. "You might want to take that off, though. It won't stay that pretty."

I am shocked when Eldorath promptly takes off his jacket, throws it over his shoulder, and heads to the pile of wood. He picks up a long plank, examines it, then throws it onto the good pile.

He does this alone for a minute while everyone watches. Tired of watching, Calvin joins him, and Eldorath gives him an appreciative smile. Slowly, when it doesn't seem like he's going to cast a spell on them, they all go back to what they were doing.

Papa hugs me. "You did a good thing," he whispers,

watching Eldorath. I look up at him, puzzled. "You did what I couldn't do," he says, and there is a quaver in his voice. "You brought him out. You brought the village together. You know, I asked him plenty of times to come to the house and have dinner, but he wouldn't. He said the neighbors wouldn't like it. That it would make life hard for us if he came. But you made him come. You did this, Clara." He turns his back on me and tells me to go continue with what I was doing, and I think it's because he doesn't want me to see him tearing up.

When the day comes to an end, Papa stands on the edge of Ms. Gee's land, thanking everyone for their hard work as they leave. Eldorath approaches him, looking completely different from the Eldorath who came here this morning. His hat is gone—he gave it to Ms. Gee, who insisted on being here to supervise everyone. His trousers are rolled to his knees, and his sleeves are rolled above his elbows. Beads of sweat fall too fast for him to wipe them all away. I don't think I've ever seen him so dirty.

He shakes Papa's hand. "You know I have the house," Eldorath says. He nods toward Ms. Gee under the guava tree. "I've told her I want her to stay with me. Her, her daughter"—he smiles over at Rudy—"the delightful Rudy. They can have the upstairs and I'll stay out of their way. Maybe we could all do with the company."

Papa pulls Eldorath into a tight hug, and for a second they stay there before they release each other.

As Eldorath leaves up the hill toward his house, Pastor Brown approaches Papa. "Is that a good idea, encouraging him?"

Papa folds his arms across his chest and opens his mouth to say something, but I butt in, "You've been making stories up about Eldorath for years now, Pastor Brown, and he hasn't said one bad thing about you. You've said he's the devil, he's evil. And all he's ever said is that he wants things to go back to the way they were before, when everyone came to his house for parties and no one thought he was a monster. He could have been angry with you for the lies you told about him, but he isn't. Even after everything, he wants to be part of this village, and I think that makes him a better person than any of us, don't you?"

My heart is beating fast, but I can't hide the pride I feel in myself. Rudy beams and gives me a thumbs-up. I said what I wanted to say, but I didn't get mad. I didn't run away.

Papa nods to me without looking away from Pastor Brown. "What my daughter said."

CHAPTER
TWENTY-FIVE

TO OUR SURPRISE, MS. GEE AGREES to Eldorath's offer
in the only way that Ms. Gee could. "If I spend another
day here, I might die of food poisoning." Mama doesn't
take offense, though. I think she is glad to see the back of
Ms. Gee.

We take her up the hill, along with Rudy and her mom.
When we get there, Eldorath is shocked to see us all, even
though it was his invitation that brought us up here.

"Well, are you going to make us stand here all day?"
Ms. Gee demands. Eldorath moves aside and lets us in.

"I wasn't expecting you all so soon. It's not ready for
visitors." He apologizes, taking us into the sitting room
with the piano. I watch Mama and Rudy's mom as they
look around the rooms in awe. Ms. Gee breaks the silence:

"It smells dusty in here. don't you clean? Open a window, open the doors, let some breeze in here."

Eldorath is reduced to a child being told off by his mother. He runs over to the door that leads out onto the balcony, pulls the curtains aside, and opens it. A stream of sunlight explodes into the room.

Now it's no longer a dark, haunting room. The sun hits the chandeliers, making shapes that dance on the ceiling. Eldorath grabs a chair at Ms. Gee's orders so she can sit outside and enjoy the sun.

I follow Eldorath as he rushes into the kitchen to make drinks. His back is turned when I lay the letters on the kitchen table. When he turns with a glass jug in hand, he stops short. He looks from the letters to me. Slowly he places the jug on the table and rests his hands on either side of the stack.

"You collected Ms. Gee's letters, didn't you? You read them to her."

A small smile pulls at his lips. "How did you know?"

I hear footsteps, and it is Rudy and Calvin joining us. Rudy picks up the letters and flicks through them.

"Calvin said that if it were any of us, we would all know, and he's right. Nothing happens in Sycamore. Nothing exciting. If Ms. Gee was getting letters from America and one of us knew about it, all of us would know."

Eldorath reaches across the table for Rudy's hand. "I tried to get her to respond. In the end, I had to do it for her."

Rudy looks up from the letters. "You wrote the letter inviting us here?"

Eldorath nodded. "Enough families have split on this hill, and all for what? For rumors? Hurt feelings?"

"So you've been visiting Ms. Gee this whole time?" Calvin asks, his eyebrows raised in surprise. "When?"

Eldorath walks to his fridge for some water and ice, then pours them into the jug with a packet of Kool-Aid.

"The same day I go to the market, I get my mail and hers. In the evening when everyone is home, I walk down and I sit with her." He stirs the mixture with a large spoon. "Sometimes I read her letters, sometimes I read her a chapter from the Bible." He glances over at our baffled faces. "Sometimes we talk about friends who haven't moved on." He grabs a silver tray and places the jug and some glasses on it. "Now help me take these in, will you? I have guests." His face is beaming with pride.

"You know, your father would throw some parties up here," Ms. Gee says, breathing in the fresh wind that none of us get farther down the hill. Rudy's mom sits on the wall, admiring the view, and I think I see her holding Ms. Gee's hand.

When I ask Rudy if Ms. Gee likes her mom now, Rudy beams, saying ever since her mom backed Ms. Gee at the party, Ms. Gee has been speaking to her more and more.

"I think she might like us," Rudy says, and I think she might be right, because Ms. Gee never lets anyone touch her without saying something about it.

"The entire town would be here, women in their best dresses, the men in their tailored suits," Ms. Gee says, waving her arm around. "The music, the dancing . . . they don't make them like that anymore." I move outside to listen. I've never heard Ms. Gee talk so excitedly about anything. There is almost a smile threatening at the edge of her lips, but I could be wrong.

"A bit of cleanup and you'll be back there again. And by cleanup, I don't just mean the dust." She points to her temple, and Eldorath chuckles.

Eldorath tells me, Rudy, and Calvin to offer everyone sandwiches and the Kool-Aid he made. Papa is already tucking in and Mama has just offered to make Ms. Gee a plate when there is a loud knock at the front door.

Eldorath looks up, startled. As if sensing his fear, Papa offers to go and see who it is. We all follow except

Ms. Gee. Papa opens the front door to find Pastor Brown, Juliette, and Uncle Albert, along with most of our neighbors, standing on the doorstep.

"Barry," Papa says, surprised. I feel someone take my hand, and it is Eldorath. "What can we do for you?"

Pastor Brown looks at me, then behind me to Eldorath. "Well," he says in that big sigh that Pastor Brown does when he's about to say something he thinks is important. "A very wise person told me we haven't been good neighbors, so we are here to rectify that."

My heart fills, and I feel as though I am about to burst. I look at Eldorath and he is in disbelief. He looks at me, then at Papa, his eyes wide.

"Well? Can we come in?"

We all turn to Eldorath. Pastor Brown wants to make amends, but it's up to Eldorath whether he wants to accept the offer. He is the one who has been suffering, after all. "Yes, yes." Eldorath ushers them in.

I see Pastor Brown nod in relief, and they enter. He opens his arms to Eldorath, and I hold my breath. Eldorath cautiously accepts his hug, and Pastor Brown pats him on the back, asking if they can see the house. Eldorath shows them around. The sitting room, the kitchen, the closet filled with clothes. At first, they are quiet and Eldorath is hesitant. But by the time they enter the closet, the house is filled with chatter as they remember the parties Eldorath's father would hold.

When they return to the sitting room, they are laughing about the trouble they would get themselves into in this house.

"We would have all sorts of adventures," Papa chuckles. Everyone gathers on the balcony with Ms. Gee, and the chatter slowly fades as they all look out into the overgrown garden that has been neglected for years.

The air feels heavy with guilt and unsaid words.

"I do love a party," Eldorath sighs, breaking the silence, and it's as if that's all they have been waiting for.

"Well, I'll need some help to cut the grass," Papa says.

Uncle Albert volunteers to get his tools.

"I can make my special cake," Juliette says in the meekest voice I have ever heard from Juliette.

"I can take care of the supplies," Pastor Brown says.

I slip one hand into Eldorath's, and with the other I take Rudy's. "We'll decorate the house."

"And the theme?" Eldorath adds. "We need a theme."

Without thinking, I blurt out, "Seventies American fashion. Seventies for you, Uncle," I say to him, "and American because that's what Gaynah would have wanted."

It is the first time I have said her name out loud in front of them all. There is a moment as everyone takes this in. I know they are thinking about Gaynah, but no one says a word. No one has to; we are all thinking the same thing. It was a year ago that it all happened, and somehow it feels like it was yesterday. It's as though by saying her name out loud, we are finally letting her go, and now the hill can move on.

CHAPTER
TWENTY-SIX

IT'S EARLY WHEN PAPA WAKES ME. The sun isn't even up. It's still dark outside. "Clara, wake up. We're going on an adventure."

I stare at him, bleary-eyed. Last time we went on an adventure, Bishop Mason told me I was crazy. Papa yanks the covers off me. "Come, it's a long drive."

Papa has borrowed Pastor Brown's car again, only this time there is no Mama, just me and Papa. When we reach town, he doesn't drive straight through the traffic circle like we did last time; he turns left along the west coast, and that's when I finally believe we are not going back to the city. He says he has a stop to make first, and he parks outside his friend's beach bar, which isn't a beach bar anymore but just an empty space.

The sand has been cleared, and you can't even tell Milo's bar was ever there before the storm. Papa shakes his head, looking around for Milo, and we spot him where the boats are always moored in the sand. When we get closer, we see that only the expensive boats have survived the storm. A mango tree has fallen on the storage hut where Milo and a few other people keep their boats. He and a few fishermen are chopping the tree up branch by branch so they can get to their boats.

Papa runs to join them, digging through the layers of mounded sand and fallen branches. I try to help as much as I can, collecting small branches and scooping sand to one side. After an hour the damage is clear to see. The boats are irreparable. It's impossible to tell that they were even boats to begin with. The damage sustained by the bigger boats, shifted from their positions as the storm tried to take them out to sea, is nothing compared to what happened to Papa's and Milo's. Now they are just broken pieces of wood lying flat in the sand.

"So, we build again," Papa says, breaking the silence as they all mourn the loss of their boats.

Milo nods with a sigh. "We build again," he agrees.

Papa pats Milo on the back. "Together."

I know Papa doesn't have the money to build a new boat, but he will beg favors from builders who know and trust him. He will offer them lobster for Christmas, or Mama's special peppered prawns, in exchange for supplies.

When we get back in the car, the mood is more somber. Papa stares vacantly at the road, his elbow on the door.

"I'm sorry, Papa," I say, knowing full well how much it hurts him every time a storm damages his boat.

He sits upright. "It's just stuff," he says. "The main thing is, we are all okay." He reaches over to the radio and switches it on. Koffee's "Toast" blasts into the car. Papa bangs the car door in appreciation. He leans his head back on the seat, singing at the top of his voice, and I join him, screaming the lyrics, arm out the window riding the breeze as we drive along the empty road.

An hour later, we slow down just before entering Bridgewater, a tourist town known for its long sandy beaches. Papa turns onto a small road that leads to the beach, and I sit up straight. Bridgewater gets busy this time of year. People come from all over the world for a week of surfing competitions.

The sun has just risen by the time we park on a small dune packed with cars. I jump out before Papa even has time to put the brakes on and run to the top of the dune. The beach is packed with surfers and spectators.

A man sits on a lifeguard post with a microphone,

commentating on the surfers out in the water. I think I might pass out with excitement. I don't know where to look first, there is so much going on.

Papa joins me. "They have a few amateur competitions," he says. "Nothing too serious, just enough to wet your feet. I put your name down for the juniors." When I don't answer, he shakes me. "You okay?"

I nod, then shake my head. I don't know. This is all too much. "They tell me we can rent boards on the other side of the beach that are a little better than the one you have at home, and you need a new suit." He checks his watch. "Your race is in twenty minutes."

I keep asking Papa if this is real. Then I ask him to pinch me so I know for sure.

"I'm not pinching you, because you'll cry and tell your mother." Instead, he pulls me into a hug, and I rest my head on his chest.

We come to a small hut with a straw roof. It is filled with people looking at boards. Papa takes my hand and forces his way through the crowd. At the back of the hut is a row of wetsuits. Papa tells me to pick one while he taps a long-haired guy on the shoulder. "Sir, my daughter needs a board. Not just any board, the coolest one you have."

I choose a fish board with pink squiggles all over it

because it reminds me of Rudy. It will be as though she is with me. Rudy would love to be here. She would be screaming at the thought of me surfing. I wish she were here to see me. I wish they all were.

I drag my board proudly along the sand, talking non-stop to Papa about what I'm going to do in the water. We stop by some beach chairs, and only then do I notice that everyone from Sycamore Hill is there, even Ms. Gee. I gasp as Mama hugs me, then Pastor Brown and Calvin, Rudy and then Eldorath. I am so happy to see him, I bury my head in his chest.

"What are you all doing here?"

"Well, your father said you had a little talent to show us," Eldorath says, and he is smiling.

"You're our daughter too," Pastor Brown adds. "We will support everything you do." His voice stumbles a little.

Mama and Juliette fuss over me, Mama fixing my wet-suit and shorts while Juliette braids my hair away from my face. Calvin helps me wax my board, and Rudy joins him. Neither of them says anything, but as we wax silently, we share this moment. Rudy nudges me and gives a small squeal, which starts Calvin chanting my name under his breath. Rudy joins him, and they both quietly chant my name while we wax the board.

I wave them away bashfully. "Stop."

The guy on the microphone announces the start of the junior amateurs, and my heart skips a beat. I feel a little sick. I've never surfed in front of an audience before, and this will be my first time getting on a board since last year.

Papa helps me to my feet. "Look how far you've come." His lips twitch.

"Papa . . ."

"I'm not crying," he says, but I'm not convinced. I look over his shoulder at a group of juniors gathering.

"Do you want me to come with you?"

"No, Papa."

I take my board over to where a boy and a girl are waiting for their turn. I stand behind the girl with short twisted hair. It's been a while since I spoke to someone new. Someone who doesn't know my past.

Part of me wants to turn and run back to Papa and Rudy, where it's safe. Another part of me desperately needs this, to start fresh. I take a deep breath and tap her shoulder.

I wave. "Hi, I'm Clara."

The girl smiles. "I'm Bridgette." She taps the boy in front of her. "This is my brother Paulton." The boy, who is at least a foot taller than both of us and has short dreads, gives me the shaka sign of hello with his thumb and a pinkie.

"I haven't seen you around here before," Paulton says. "You new?"

"I surf with friends in Sycamore," I tell him. Does he need to know one of my friends was a ghost and I've only just said goodbye to her? Not yet.

"Cool," he says. "I've done most of the island, but not Sycamore. Are the waves good?"

Before I can answer, my name is called. I tell them we'll talk later, and something feels good about saying that. They both pat me on the back, wishing me luck.

As I run toward the water, I can hear Mama and Papa cheering me on. I blow out air to calm my nerves, wading into the water, trying to block out the emcee's commentary.

You can do this, Clara.

I slide onto the board and paddle out. When I am far enough out, I sit and wait for the wave.

"Yay, Clara!"

I turn toward the beach, where Rudy is waving excitedly. She cups her hands around her mouth. "You're a surfing warrior!" she screams. "You're a surfing warrior with wings, and the wave is your enemy."

It's all I need. I turn back to the sea as a wave hurtles

toward me. My heart is pounding against my chest; my ears are filled with the sound of Rudy chanting my name. I wait until the last second, jump on my feet, and turn my board along the inside of the wave. The moment lasts only seconds before I fall off my board.

But I have never felt more alive.

ACKNOWLEDGMENTS

When I first sat down to write this story, I had no idea where it was going. All I knew was I wanted to write about friendships. How losing your best friend can be the worst heartbreak in the world but also how important it is to have good people in your life.

What I ended up with was much more than that. Clara's story became part of me. Her town is where I was born. Pick leaf is a game I played as a child. Her story will always be special to me.

None of this would have been possible without the following people, who have believed in me, motivated me, and worked tirelessly to get Clara's story into the world.

To Alice, agent extraordinaire. Thank you for taking a chance on me. Thank you for fighting in my corner. You have changed my life. To everyone at the Madeleine Milburn Agency, who work so hard for their clients, thank you.

Thank you to my US editor, Kelsey Horton, and to the entire Delacorte Press team, who have turned my vision into reality. Thank you for sharing my enthusiasm and love for Clara's story.

To my UK publishers, Pushkin Press, especially my

editor, Sarah, thank you for your ongoing support whenever I have needed it. Thank you for sharing my vision.

To my son, Tristan, who threatened to press send on my manuscript when I was too scared to do it myself because "They're going to love it, Mum." I cherish the moments when we laugh about the silliest things, when you trust me with your fears and your goals. You are going to be a force in this world.

To my sister, Karen, who has seen me through the roughest times, making everything bearable with impromptu day trips and holding my hand whenever I needed it, thank you.

To my mum, Makeda, who patiently listened to every high and every low and responded with "But you always do it, even when you're afraid." Thank you for always having my back.

To Lynda Mason, who has been my cheerleader from day one. Thank you for believing in me when I often (daily) didn't believe in myself. Here's to more adventures.

To Mrs. Henson, my English teacher who told me to do something with my writing and never got to see this book for herself.

Thank you to the *Nottingham Review* for publishing my first-ever short story and to Ad Hoc fiction for nominating my story for Best Short Fiction.

Thank you to the FAB Awards for shining a light on writers of color. To #DVpit, which gives underrepresented voices a chance to shine and is the reason I met my agent. To all the writing friends I made on Twitter, and especially to those on Instagram who have supported my poetry and short stories from the beginning. Thank you.

From the author of the critically acclaimed *When Life Gives You Mangos*, a poignant coming-of-age story about a girl who is gifted surprise letters from her late mother. Reading them might change everything.

Turn the page for a preview of
Kereen Getten's new novel.

THE NIGHT BEFORE MY BIRTHDAY, MAMA would always slip a note under my door. It would read:

Dear Ms. Brie,
Thank you for staying at the Wonderland Hotel. We want to give you the experience of a lifetime, so to begin, please check your choices for breakfast in the morning:

- CEREAL
- PORRIDGE
- FRUIT: MANGO
- FRUIT: BANANA
- FRUIT: PINEAPPLE
- FRUIT: ALL THREE
- EGG SCRAMBLED
- EGG FRIED
- EGG OMELET
- ALL THREE

- BACON
- SAUSAGE
- PLANTAIN
- ACKEE & SALTFISH
- TEA
- HOT CHOCOLATE
- MILO
- ORANGE JUICE
- WATER

After Mama died, and after I could think about her again without crying, I started slipping Mama's menu under Nana's door the night before my birthday. Every year, I listen for her to go to bed, and giggle under my pillow when she finds it. "What is this? This girl really takes me for a hotel." But every morning for the last three years, I've woken to the smell of breakfast, and all the foods on my list.

That's Nana. Always making a fuss when I ask her for something but doing it anyway.

This morning, though, I don't smell the food I asked for. So I jump out of bed to see if Nana got my note last night.

The new frilly dress she forces me to wear every year is hanging on the back of the door. I ignore it and throw on one of my nicer tops and a pair of black shorts instead.

When I come out of my room, I can hear voices and the faint sound of music. I enter the living room from the hallway and peer to the left into the small kitchen at the back of the house. The walls are bright pink, painted over from when Mama woke one day and painted the entire kitchen because she saw it in a dream. She and Papa argued that day. He said no one painted their kitchen pink, and it made his head hurt. Mama said, "Then we will be the first, and your head will get used to it."

From the living room, I can see Nana bustling around with her back to me. She's wearing a long pink dress that is supposed to match my frilly one. Hers makes her look like an overgrown doll, but for some reason Nana likes to find us matching clothes for special occasions.

"Nana?" I call, entering the kitchen. I look around, confused. There is no food. The table is empty. Maybe she's finally had enough of my requests.

She spins around, surprised. "What are you doing up?" she cries, then peers out the window before returning her gaze to me. Her long white hair sits on her shoulders, styled in the big curls she always wears when she dresses up. Nana has had the same hairstyle since I was born, and before, because I've seen photos of her back in the 1800s and her hair was the same then too. She's tried to put makeup on over the usually bare skin, but Nana isn't very good at makeup and her eyeliner makes her look like a pirate.

I frown. "It's what people do in the morning, Nana. They wake up."

She looks around, distracted, "Yes . . . yes, they do, but you think you can go back?"

I stare at her. "Go back?"

She nods, glancing out the window. "Yes, maybe go and change into that dress I left out for you."

I point down to what I'm wearing. "Nana, I can't do the six-year-old Sunday-school look anymore."

She looks at me, exasperated. "You can't make your Nana happy this one time, Brie? I'm an old woman and I only have one wish."

I let out a loud groan, throwing my face to the ceiling. "Nooooo, not the last-wish blackmail."

She fidgets with the tray in her hand. "It's just a dress."

"It's an embarrassment to dresses. All the other dresses disowned it. Even the shop owner didn't want it in the shop no more." I continue to moan about the dress, but she has already turned away.

"Put the dress on, Brie."

"The lady who made it threw it away because she regretted making it."

"Bridgette . . ."

"I bet there's a petition on social media demanding that this dress never be seen by human eyes."

"All I ask from you is one thing. . . ."

"I'll die. The dress will kill me. I . . . can't . . . breathe. . . ." I pretend to collapse.

Aunty Elsa, Papa's sister, appears in the doorway, eyes beaming. "Brie," she says, surprised, then turns to Nana and whispers, "We're ready."

Nana heads toward the back door. She looks over her shoulder at me. "Brie, put on the dress. I'm not going to ask you again."

I drag my feet back to the room and stare at the frilly pink dress hanging on the back of the door. I sigh and take it off the hanger. At least it's only Nana and Papa seeing me in this dress. It could be worse—the whole town could see me wearing it.

❄❄❄

"Happy birthday!" a chorus of voices shouts in unison. I step outside to lots of familiar faces looking back at me. Everyone is here. My two best friends—Smiley and Femi—and their parents; Dion, my neighbor; and Dion's three younger brothers, all wearing the same white shirt, bow tie, and blue jeans because their parents couldn't be bothered to buy them different clothes. Aunty Elsa, Papa's sister, and her boyfriend, Julius. There are more neighbors, and people from school who I barely speak to but Nana thinks are my friends because they're on my football team.

Our back garden has been transformed with fairy lights and balloons in the trees. A long table covered with pink and white cloth is filled with food, drinks, and a three-tier cake covered in pink icing. White chairs line the long table, and a separate, smaller table to the left is piled high with presents. But all I can see are people. People now staring back at me in my pink frilly dress. I feel sick.

Great. As if my life couldn't get any worse. I edge backward toward the house, but Nana reaches for my arm and links hers with mine.

"Nuh-uh. Don't you dare," she says through clenched teeth, forcing me to stay until they finish singing.

"Speech!" Julius shouts, and Aunty Elsa elbows him.

I close my eyes, hoping that when I open them this will all have been a dream. I hate attention. I can see the expectations as people wait for me to say something nice, when all I want to do is run.

I clear my throat, wishing to clear my backyard of all these people, but no. They're still here. "Nana made me wear it," I say, pointing to the dress and the shoes.

An awkward silence falls among them except for a snort from Uncle Julius. Nana turns to the sea of bemused faces. "Everyone take a seat before the food gets cold," she announces. They all sit down at the long table, while I am still rooted to the step.

Nana shoots me a look. "What's wrong with you?"

I want to tell her that if she hadn't forced me to wear the dress, none of this would have happened. Better still, if she hadn't invited the entire neighborhood, she wouldn't feel so humiliated right now.

"Go and sit down and act like you want to be here," she says, before painting on a smile and asking everyone if they need anything.

I find a spot between Smiley and Femi and sit down, grateful that at least the table hides most of the outfit.

The table is buzzing with chatter as the sun rises higher behind us. Jackfruit, the local tourist guide, is playing music from five hundred years ago, and Nana is hobbling around the table with her bad hip.

"Cool speech, Brie," Dion says from across the table. My face gets hot, and I nearly choke on my pineapple. It's not that Dion and I have never talked—we used to talk all the time. Mama would take him to nursery with me when we were small, but then we got older, and he became cool and popular and I didn't. He got new friends and we grew apart.

We're so different now. I cringe when I think about the days I used to make him dress up as a doll and play make-believe.

Smiley nudges me under the table. "Don't ignore him," she hisses behind her hand. "Say something back."

I purse my lips at her before switching to a smile when I realize Dion is looking.

"Thank you for not coming," I blurt out.

Smiley and Femi snort with laughter on either side of me.

As the table empties, Aunty Elsa approaches me from behind. "You ready for your presents?"

This is my favorite part of my birthday. Not because I expect big, expensive things—we don't have enough money for that. This is when I get to see if Nana and Papa have picked up on any of my hints in the past six months. It also means I don't have to stand in front of everyone again in this dress.

What I really want is a better phone so I won't get laughed at anymore at school or want to hide it in my pocket when someone calls me. I only got a phone three years ago because Nana wanted a way to contact me if she was going to be late picking me up from school.

I wrap my arms around myself and follow her over to the smaller table. "Where's Papa?" I ask, suddenly realizing he is not in the crowd.

"He had to rush into work," Aunty Elsa tells me, "but he'll be back soon." My heart sinks, and I try to hide how disappointed I am that he can't even be here for my birthday. I should be used to this now. This isn't new; this is all the time. If it isn't my birthday, it's the school play or sports day at school. Papa is rarely around: work is always more important than me.

I feel Aunty Elsa's arm around my shoulder. "He'll be here," she whispers in my ear. I push down the knot in my throat. Swallowing it hurts every time as though it's the first time. I'm embarrassed and hurt that Papa can't take a few hours off for my birthday. Aunty Elsa and Julius could do it; even our neighbors could be here. But not Papa. It's as if spending time with me is the hardest thing for him.

I take a deep breath and bite my lip as Nana joins us at the table. She and Aunty Elsa surround me, kissing my face and stroking my hair, neither of them saying a word, but I know what they're telling me—that it's okay.

Nana picks up a small box covered with silver wrapping paper and hands it to me. "Right, this one first," she says. She beams at me the way Nana does when she wants me to do the same, to smile.

So I do what she asks: I force a smile that hides my disappointment.

"It's from your father," Nana says, "to store things in. He bought it from the wood carver on the beach." I stare inside the box and wonder when he found the time to get this when he barely has time for me. Maybe, just like for Christmas and other people's birthdays, he gives Nana a list so she can buy presents for him.

"It's nice," I murmur.

"Pick ours next," Julius calls from the table. Aunty Elsa glares at him. "What?" he says, throwing his hands in the air. "She just opened an empty box. Ours will look like gold." He chuckles to himself but stops abruptly when Nana shoots him a look.

Nana hands me presents one by one, and the morning moves slowly, like when you're in your last class at school and the clock doesn't seem to move.

Nana has a story for every present, or she forces whoever bought the present to stand up and tell everyone why they chose it, and I wish she wouldn't talk so long. I wish she wouldn't make such a big deal over every present. I don't understand why everyone is here. Half these people weren't here for my eleventh birthday or my tenth, so why are they here now? Why this birthday? What's the big deal about being twelve?

Her voice swims in and out like a wave and I try to focus. I try to smile, and I try to remember to say thank you for every present I open. But my heart isn't in it because Papa isn't here.

I get a hamper basket from Smiley and Femi, filled with all my favorite chocolates and a bag of tamarind balls. A locket with a photo of the family, including Mama, from Uncle Julius and Aunty Elsa. The photo is old. I look about three years old in it, and Papa is smiling, so I know it's old. I stare at the photo, remembering how things changed so much after Mama died. How one day everything was perfect and then it wasn't.

"Thank you, Aunty Elsa and Uncle Julius."

Dion's mother gets me perfume. Nana gets me a pair of white sneakers. "The lady at the shop says all the kids are wearing them," she says, nodding to the box in my hand. I see movement from the corner of my eye and look up expecting to see Papa, but it's not; it's Uncle Julius getting more food. I return my empty gaze to the shoebox.

"Thanks, Nana," I mumble without looking up.

I'm hoping this is it and Nana will send everyone home so I can stop pretending.

"There's one more," Nana says, and my heart sinks. She looks over to the house, frowning. "Where's your father? He's supposed to be here for this."

"I'll call him," Julius says, taking out his phone and walking away from the table. We wait in silence as he calls Papa's phone, Nana with the box in her hand and Aunty Elsa with her arms tightly around my shoulder. We all wait in silence except for Dion's three brothers, who start hitting each other. Julius turns and shakes his head, slipping the phone back in his pocket. "Some emergency at work," he says, giving me a quick, reassuring smile. "He says to carry on but he will be here as soon as he can."

The embarrassment of what people must be thinking weighs heavy. I can imagine what they are saying under their breath. *Why isn't he here? It's her birthday.* I avoid their eyes so I can't see what they are thinking. I twist my fingers to stop myself from feeling.

Nana sighs, exchanging a look with Aunty Elsa before her eyes lower to the box in her hand. I feel Aunty Elsa's fingers pressing into my skin. I feel her body stiffen beside me and I look at her. She forces a smile, stroking my shoulder, but her eyes are misty, as though she is about to cry. I'm confused why Aunty Elsa is so upset about Papa not being here.

Nana picks up the box, but instead of handing it to me, she holds it close to her chest. She pauses, then looks over at Aunty Elsa next to me. "If her father isn't here to do it, then it should be you." Aunty Elsa lets go of me and moves over to Nana and takes the box. They both look at me with a look I have seen so many times, the one that says *Poor girl, poor Brie*. I feel a knot in my stomach, and I press my hands into the fold of my dress.

"This," Aunty Elsa says, looking down at the box. "This is from your mama." And it's as if I lose my breath.